"I have plans for this place that I'm not prepared to give up on."

"I understand," Sawyer said. "I really do. I'm just looking for the best way to help my daughter."

Their words hung between them like an opaque curtain.

Doctor Burgess came out of her office, explaining that there'd been an incident with her mother at the care home where she lived. "It's getting harder to juggle things, though. I really do need to find a buyer for this clinic sooner rather than later."

Panic shot through Bridget, and Sawyer avoided making eye contact with her.

Bridget resolved then that she would do her job and be civil with Sawyer. She would make sure that his daughter felt welcome.

But she wouldn't let herself forget, not for one second, that Sawyer was her rival and that they both had an eye on the same property.

No matter how appealing his obvious love for his daughter made him.

Donna Gartshore loves reading and writing. She also writes short stories, poetry and devotionals. She often veers off to the book section in the grocery store when she should be buying food. Besides talking about books and writing, Donna loves spending time with her daughter, Sunday family suppers and engaging online with the writing community.

Books by Donna Gartshore

Love Inspired

Instant Family
Instant Father
Finding Her Voice

Visit the Author Profile page at LoveInspired.com.

Finding Her Voice

Donna Gartshore

LOVE INSPIRED
INSPIRATIONAL ROMANCE

LOVE INSPIRED®

INSPIRATIONAL ROMANCE

PLEASE RECYCLE • THIS PRODUCT IS RECYCLABLE •

Recycling programs for this product may not exist in your area.

ISBN-13: 978-1-335-58600-1

Finding Her Voice

Copyright © 2022 by Donna Lynn Gartshore

For questions and comments about the quality of this book, please contact us at CustomerService@Harlequin.com.

Love Inspired
22 Adelaide St. West, 41st Floor
Toronto, Ontario M5H 4E3, Canada
www.LoveInspired.com

Printed in U.S.A.

And we know that all things work together for good to them that love God, to them who are the called according to his purpose.

—*Romans* 8:28

As always for my daughter—
I hope to make her as proud as she makes me.

To my mom and sisters—love our daily texts!
Thank you for your ongoing love and support.

A special shout-out to the real Sophie and to
Stan making a cameo appearance as Mr. Snow.

Thank you to my editor, Melissa Endlich,
and my agent, Tamela Hancock Murray.
It's a pleasure to work with you
and I appreciate you both.

And, not least, to God, Who gifts me with
creativity and gives me the courage to use it,
for which I am endlessly grateful.

Chapter One

"Bridget, I'm going for a quick lunch." Dr. Doris Burgess popped her head out of her office, on a Monday morning in early July. The intelligent, straightforward Indigenous woman had been the veterinarian in Green Valley, Saskatchewan, for many years, and as Dr. Burgess's early retirement neared, Bridget was aware of how much she was going to miss the fifty-five-year-old veterinarian.

They worked well together and, although Bridget was still pursuing her animal psychology degree by taking online classes and was still the clinic's receptionist, her boss was supportive of her goal, which was to start a program to match abandoned animals with people who would derive benefit from having a pet.

"Trust you can manage things?" Her gaze surveyed the interior of the Green Valley Animal Clinic, empty except for the golden retriever that Bridget had found abandoned on the highway between the city of Regina, Saskatchewan, and the small town of Green Valley, where she lived. Two weeks and numerous phone calls had failed to bring an owner forward. Bridget couldn't bear to take the already traumatizeddog to a shelter, so she'd brought her into her own home.

"I'll be fine, take your time." Bridget smiled brightly and did her best to ignore the knot of tension that threaded through her body.

Part of the tension was a perpetual state ever since she had dated and broken up with Wes. Memories of the abusive relationship still lingered, and, despite making strides with the help of the support group she attended, she feared they would never completely go away. But now, added to that, she didn't know what the future held for her career. She knew that Doc B was looking for someone to buy or invest in the clinic. Her dream was to come up with enough money to make a down payment on the clinic. It would not only keep the clinic open—she'd also be one step closer to achieving her own goal.

Her stomach turned at the thought of losing the opportunity. She had always loved her job, but after Wes it had become more than employment to her. It was a place where she could focus on something other than regret and shame.

The logical part of her knew that being a victim of abuse was nothing to be ashamed of, but the emotional scars remained.

Bridget couldn't blame Doc Burgess for announcing her retirement and her intention to sell the clinic. She simply couldn't compete with new animal clinics that were only a short drive away and able to offer twenty-four-hour service, as well as the latest in technology to diagnose illnesses. It was just a shame that people appeared to value convenience over loyalty these days. With such a large staff and client list, those places surely couldn't offer the kind of heart and personal attention that Dr. Burgess provided. She truly knew her clients and their pets' histories.

If only Bridget could move toward her degree in animal psychology at a faster pace, but she needed to keep working so could only take classes online part-time. She chose not to tell Dr. Burgess that she wanted to make an offer to purchase the clinic herself, not until she'd talked to the bank to see if a loan was possible. But she needed to have a solid plan in place to present to them, to come across in an assured and professional manner to convince them that she was worth taking a risk on.

Nerves brought about by the fear of them saying no was causing her to procrastinate on asking the bank for the loan, but Bridget knew she had to do something soon before someone else came along and scooped the opportunity out from under her. The clinic was on a premium piece of property, a great central location that would entice many buyers.

She squared her shoulders. She would do this; she had to. Keeping the clinic operational so that she could pursue her own dreams was an important step in becoming the brand-new Bridget she needed to become if she was going to leave the scars of what had happened to her behind. Maybe that way she could stop thinking about how she'd stayed in a toxic relationship for far too long. There had to be some good that could come out of such a horrid experience. If she stopped believing that, she didn't know what she would do.

"We'll hold the fort, won't we, Sophie?" Bridget said.

The dog rolled her eyes and whimpered low in her throat.

"It's okay, girl." Bridget scratched behind Sophie's soft, feathery ears. "No pressure." She was reassuring herself as much as the dog.

"Can I bring you anything back?" Dr. Burgess asked.

"No, thanks."

"Okay. I won't be long," the doctor said. "Oh,

by the way, the computer where the auditor is supposed to be working is acting up again. There seems to be a few glitches with the new software."

"I can take a look," Bridget said.

She was glad to have something to do instead of having too much time to think, too much time to imagine the door swinging open and Wes bursting in with that arrogant stride of his and that particular glint in his eye. He still caused bad dreams that made her suddenly bolt up in bed, trembling as she fumbled to turn on the lamp, and take deep breaths as she reminded herself that those days were over.

Yet, even knowing that he had moved to Vancouver, she watched for him everywhere, her body a perpetual knot of tightness.

It was her turn to speak at the Tuesday-night meeting of the Women's Survivors of Abuse Anonymous group she attended so, after she tried to diagnose the software problem, and if no clients came in, she could focus on jotting some notes for that. It was a great place to unburden and maybe one day she would find the courage to tell those closest to her what she had gone through. But, so far, she hadn't even told Charlotte Belvedere, her cousin and best friend.

She couldn't imagine ever telling her parents,

who, because of past griefs, longed only for life to be pleasant and positive.

But Bridget was ever grateful to Mavis, an active member in the abuse support group she attended, who had sensed something despite Bridget's insistent denials, and was persistent in her quest to get Bridget to a meeting. Mavis, whose son was one of Charlotte's former students, had experienced her own painful journey out of an abusive marriage.

"Speaking of the auditor," Dr. Burgess said, pausing in the doorway, "he should be arriving from Saskatoon tomorrow."

"Okay," Bridget said. Her stomach lurched at the thought of the auditor coming across something that would get in the way of her plan. She had to get to the bank sooner rather than later. No more procrastinating, she told herself.

Well, she would simply have to pray that didn't happen, even though her prayers often felt dry and empty since her relationship with Wes.

She believed in God, and she tried to believe that He had a plan and purpose for what she'd gone through, but it wasn't easy.

After Dr. Burgess left for lunch, Sophie, as if picking up on Bridget's pensive mood, pressed closer to her and whined. But the sound was muffled by a wad of gauze hanging halfway out of Sophie's mouth and puffing out her cheeks.

Bridget shook her head at the dog, but couldn't help smiling. "When did you manage to pick that up?" The retriever's compulsion to always have something in her mouth amused her.

Sophie's entire back end twitched into a joyful wag.

"What am I going to do with you?" Bridget asked, gently retrieving the gauze and scratching behind the dog's ears. Sophie flopped down and grunted as if to say she had no idea. Bridget had made some progress with Sophie since rescuing her but the dog was still a furry bundle of nerves with most people.

"Come on, let's have another look at that computer," Bridget said and Sophie happily followed her into one of the offices.

Bridget sat down at the computer and clicked on the recently installed software. It loaded, but only after a long wait.

"Yup, it's definitely slowing things down," she murmured. They would either have to increase the internet speed or free up some space on the computer, but she didn't want to delete files without Doc B's input.

There wasn't much else she could do at the moment, so she and Sophie went back to the reception area.

She had just finished guiding Sophie to some more appropriate chew toys when the door banged open. Habitually, she braced to see Wes, even knowing how unlikely that was. She lifted her chin and folded her arms in front of her. But then she let out the breath she'd been holding and tilted her head sideways to study the new arrival. Sophie mimicked the action.

The little girl was wearing pink shorts that were slightly baggy on her and a pink-and-blue-and-white-flowered blouse. She had denim-blue eyes and light brown hair that was stick straight and just brushed her shoulders. Her bangs were in a fringe across her forehead. She was cute, and her bone structure made it likely that she would grow into a beauty as she matured.

She couldn't have been more than seven or eight years old, so why was she alone?

The little girl spotted Sophie and headed straight for her.

"Careful!" Bridget warned. "She's nervous around people and sometimes she…" But before she could get the words out, the little girl was squatting in front of Sophie, tickling under her chin and whispering into her ear.

Bridget was studying the profound effects that humans and animals could have on one another but witnessing it was something altogether different.

"There's a good girl. You're a good girl," the little girl said and Sophie half closed her eyes, basking in the attention and thumping her tail like she'd found her new best friend.

"She likes me," the girl added. Her voice was still barely louder than a whisper, like she had a sore throat or something. She gave a satisfied nod and resumed patting and whispering to Sophie, who dropped to the floor and trustingly exposed her belly.

Bridget was about to ask where her parents were when the door banged open and a man frantically stormed in, causing Bridget to take two steps backward and lock her arms across her chest again.

She silently begged God for the umpteenth time to help her stop being so afraid.

The man spotted the little girl. "Delilah!" he said. "How many times do I have to tell you not to run away like that, especially when we're in a strange place?"

It was obvious that the man was the little girl's father, or at the least a close relative, by the denim-blue eyes they shared—his framed by glasses that only added to his overall appeal— and the strong bone structure of their faces. He wore dark-wash blue jeans and a short-sleeved blue-and-gray-plaid shirt. He strode toward Delilah and raked a hand through dark blond hair that looked like it would wave or curl if it wasn't cut short.

Sophie, timid again, tucked in her hind end and hurriedly crept for safety into one of the back rooms.

Behind the receptionist's desk, Bridget watched anxiously to see what would happen. The man looked pretty agitated about things.

Delilah, however, didn't appear to be intimidated by him. She mimicked Bridget's arms-folded pose and tightened her lips, as mutiny further darkened her eyes.

"We have to get going," the man said. "Now, please, Delilah."

Bridget had no idea that there was such a thing as a tantrum with no sound, but all evidence showed that was exactly what she was witnessing. Delilah scrunched her face into a mask of anger, she clenched her fists at her side, her body went completely rigid and began to tremble and her skin took on a deepening shade of red.

"Delilah." The man spoke in a low, calm voice as he knelt down beside her. "Listen, just breathe and listen." He didn't touch her but instead reached into his pocket and pulled out his phone. He swiped a screen, pushed a button and a piece of classical music began to pour out. "Okay, Delilah," he continued in the same calm voice. "There are four layers in the melody of this song. I want you to listen and when you hear a new layer come in I want you to count it off on your fingers."

Delilah continued to shake but not quite as much.

"Okay, listen, here's one and do you hear the violins coming in? Is that…?"

She held up two fingers and he nodded. "Good, that's good! Keep listening."

An energetic swell of the brass section followed by percussion swooped in and Delilah held up a third and fourth finger. Her coloring and posture softened; her head bent in concentration.

Bridget had never seen anything like it.

The man looked up over Delilah's head and met her eyes. There was something in his gaze that tightened her stomach in wary but undeniable curiosity about who this man and his little girl were.

And if there was a mother in the picture, where was she?

"Music appreciation, senior year," he said.

"Pardon me?" Bridget found her voice.

"We learned to identify how many layers there were in a melody. Once I got into the habit of doing it, I couldn't stop." He tilted his head at the little girl. "My daughter's even better at it than I am, aren't you, Dee-Dee?"

Tantrum over, Delilah nodded and went over to look at a rack of brochures.

Well, that was all very interesting but Bridget still had no idea who they were or why they were in the clinic.

But she reminded herself that she did have duties as a receptionist. "May I help you?" she asked.

The man looked around and said, "Huh, this is kind of funny."

"What is?" Bridget asked.

"I just realized this is where I'm going to be working for the next little while. At least, I assume this is the only veterinarian in town?"

"It is," Bridget said slowly, as an unwelcome realization dawned on her.

The man smiled, bringing light to his face and making it even more striking, something she didn't want to notice but did. His glasses had slipped a little while he looked for music on his phone and he used a finger to push them back up.

"Sawyer Blume." He extended his hand in greeting. "I'll be auditing the books here. Dr. Burgess promised me there'd be someone here who could assist me with what I needed. You must be her."

Sawyer credited his business training and his family's insistence on decorum for being able to keep a facade of calm while anxiety continued to gnaw at his stomach over Delilah's brief but heart-stopping disappearance.

There was no doubt that he and Delilah needed a change if they were going to get past their grief and move forward. There were simply too many memories bogging them down in Saskatoon. Sorrow did strange and twisting things to time, so that the year since his wife Tina's sudden death seemed both endless and brief.

This was an audit that he knew shouldn't take more than a few days, a week at most. Still he welcomed the brief reprieve from the day-to-day dealings with his father and his older brother, Marc, and the family business of investing and developing properties—a business that he was having an increasingly hard time relating to. Besides the emotional turmoil, which could still be overwhelming, there was the fact that he simply didn't like the way his family worked. He couldn't remember exactly when it had become obvious that their investment company had become more about the money than about the people, but that wasn't how he wanted things to be. He had accepted this small-town audit just as his brother and father were getting geared up for a potential deal with what would be their biggest client yet. His decision to leave at such a time was definitely not a popular choice.

His father's parting words still rang a discordant note in his ears. "I don't appreciate this, Sawyer, not at all. We've got until the end of August to settle this deal and I expect you to get back here as quickly as possible. Otherwise, I'll have to draw the conclusion that you no longer care about what's right for the family."

Sawyer supposed his father had done his best to offer his version of solace after Tina's passing, but to him caring for family meant providing for them and that was where his primary focus was. But the guilt he was fed along with those words tasted bitter and he pushed them to the back of his mind, intending to focus only on what he would discover over the next few days.

But, Lord, please, if there is a way to make the changes that need to be made, if there's some way that the days ahead don't have to seem so bleak and endless, please let me know. For Delilah's sake, please.

School was out for the summer and Delilah had been struggling—with school, with so many things. A change of scenery, perhaps a whole new start, was imperative for them both. It wouldn't solve everything, Sawyer knew, but it could be an important step toward helping them process their grief.

In their correspondence, Dr. Burgess had mentioned to him that she was seeking a purchaser for the clinic. The idea lingered tantalizingly in the back of his mind, but he was unable to completely dismiss his father's words.

His father had built his successful business from the ground up and he had put heart and soul into teaching his sons every aspect of it. There had been a time when Sawyer never would have questioned or doubted what he was meant to do with his life.

But his wife's sudden death had changed that. Now he was filled with nothing but doubts and unanswered questions.

What was most important at the moment, however, was to take his daughter home—or to what they would call home while they were here—and have time to regroup before the real work started.

"I'm sure you'll find everything is in good order here," the woman said in a determined voice. Sawyer noted that the name tag she wore pinned to her light blue jacket read Bridget Connelly, a concession to strangers like him, since he assumed, by the size of the town, that the people who lived there would know who she was.

She was pretty, in a blue-eyed, blonde, natural way, and he could imagine how stunning she would be when she smiled, which she was most determinedly not doing at the moment. Even though logic told him that she couldn't have anything against him because they'd just met, she practically radiated aversion to his presence. Well, he knew that audits were never easy for employees.

So, why did he think it was something more?

His eyes scanned the office, assessing. It was spacious and clean and, from what he could tell, appeared to be in an ideal location. He allowed his imagination to wander. There was definite potential to open shop here. Of course, he would need to get to know the rest of the town, what people were like and what they were looking for, because if he did open his investment business, he wanted it to be about helping others who couldn't do it on their own, not just about making money.

He sighed. Imagining what could be was all well and good, but he still had other responsibilities.

"Can I see the dog again before we leave?" Delilah whispered.

The sound of his daughter's voice sent a fissure of emotion through Sawyer, hitting him bone-deep. He didn't know what this Bridget thought of Delilah's whisper, but she wouldn't know what a gift it was to hear her voice at all. He had entered the clinic in such a panic he hadn't stopped to consider the significance of his daughter conversing with a stranger. But now he did, so he nodded and said, "If Ms. Connelly doesn't mind. But just for a few minutes."

At the sound of her name, Bridget's eyebrows arched questioningly but then her fingers instinctively touched her name tag.

"I'll go get her," she said. "Her name is Sophie. She's a golden retriever. She's usually very shy with people." Her gaze fell on Sawyer, then on Delilah again. "So, it's nice that you were able to make friends with her."

Bridget coaxed the timid dog back out again and she crept by Sawyer with her head down, turning it only briefly with an affronted gaze that echoed Bridget's. But when she spotted Delilah her tail whirred into motion, a furry windmill, and she barked with excitement.

Sawyer thoughtfully tapped a finger on his chin, noticing the impact this dog and his little girl had on each other.

"Indoor voice, please," Bridget scolded with a wry look and Delilah smiled. Her smile was a lovely, slowly blossoming thing, but these days Sawyer saw it so rarely that its appearance twisted his heart.

"Okay," he said, brusque because he didn't want to deal with his turbulent emotions. "Five more minutes and then we have to go. Miss Price is expecting us."

"Oh, are you staying at Mildred Price's?" Bridget asked, her demeanor softening slightly.

"Yes, Dr. Burgess says she takes in boarders if needed for short periods of time and she highly recommended her."

"Mildred is a wonderful woman," Bridget assured him. "She's the best caregiver in town for the children. She's actually kind of a motherly figure to the whole town."

"That was another deciding factor," Sawyer said. "I wanted someone with experience to care for Delilah while I'm working."

He drummed his fingers at the side of his leg, not wanting to give voice to his fears, especially not to this woman, who set him off-balance in a way he didn't quite understand.

"Delilah is welcome to visit Sophie anytime, if it's all right with you," Bridget said. "Sophie is a rescue dog, abandoned by her owners, and she's still skittish, so she doesn't like to be left at home alone. Dr. Burgess doesn't mind her hanging out at work with me. In Green Valley, we look out for each other."

"You've lived here for a while, then?" Sawyer asked. His urge to get going was replaced by his curiosity about Green Valley and its potential for him and Delilah.

His daughter, sensing a shift in the atmosphere, drifted back in Sophie's direction.

"My whole life," Bridget confirmed. "I've been working here since I graduated high school."

"So you'd say Green Valley has things to offer?"

"It depends on what you're looking for, I guess." Caution crept back into Bridget's tone. She paused. "What *are* you looking for?"

"A change," Sawyer answered, surprising himself. But it felt good to say the words out loud and it was easier to say them to a stranger. *Well, in for a penny, in for a pound*, as his grandmother used to say. "I'm actually giving some thought to buying this business. I understand from Dr. Burgess that it's for sale."

The words tasted strange but welcome on his tongue. He pushed away the thought of his father's disapproval.

Bright blue eyes spit fire at Sawyer, taking him aback. "Oh, I'm quite sure that Doc B intends to sell it to someone local, someone who really knows the community."

"I didn't get that impression when I talked to her," Sawyer replied. "She just mentioned that she was looking for a buyer."

"Well, as a matter of fact..." Bridget's voice wavered slightly, then with a determination that he couldn't help but admire, she steeled herself and said, "As a matter of fact, I am planning to make an offer to buy the clinic."

Her blue eyes darted slightly to the side, then returned to focus resolutely on his.

"I'm sure Dr. Burgess will do what she thinks is best," Sawyer said. He didn't want to get into an argument or upset this undeniably attractive woman, who he sensed was troubled for reasons that he couldn't and didn't want to understand.

"I'm sure she will." She studied him a moment longer, giving him the distinct impression that he fell short in all possible areas that anyone could fall short in, and then turned abruptly away.

Sensing the tension that had sprung up in the room, Delilah stopped scratching Sophie's ears and went to Sawyer, pressing herself into his side. His arm went protectively around her. He couldn't help noticing the way Bridget's steely expression softened when she looked at his daughter.

"Your daughter is still welcome to visit Sophie anytime," Bridget said.

"That's a nice offer," Sawyer said, understanding full well that her concession was in no way extending an olive branch to him. "I'm sure we'll take you up on it. Delilah, please thank Ms. Connelly."

Delilah smiled and waggled her fingers in Bridget's direction, before darting back to Sophie and flinging her arms around the dog's neck to say goodbye. Then she tucked her hand into his and they departed, with her humming under her breath the classical piece he had played for her earlier.

He savored these moments with his daughter especially knowing now how quickly things could go sideways. Delilah wasn't the same little girl after her mother's sudden death.

But, Lord, how could she be? Sawyer asked again in the endless round of questions that never seemed to get answered. *How could You let a little girl go through that? Why didn't You protect her from what she saw?*

He wondered sometimes why he continued to pray when often nothing but an echoing silence answered him. But the thought of not praying was worse.

He couldn't help wondering exactly what Bridget's story was and how big an obstacle she was going to play in him getting what he wanted. Because, one way or the other, life couldn't go on for Delilah and him the way it was now.

Chapter Two

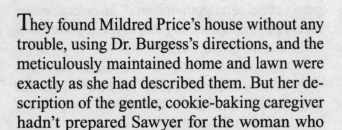

They found Mildred Price's house without any trouble, using Dr. Burgess's directions, and the meticulously maintained home and lawn were exactly as she had described them. But her description of the gentle, cookie-baking caregiver hadn't prepared Sawyer for the woman who came out the door to greet them.

Instead of the snowy-haired, frilly-aproned grandmother figure that he had pictured, Mildred Price was over six feet tall, wore overalls that looked well lived in and her white hair was in two long braids. Beside him, he felt Delilah stiffen and her small, bitten nails scraped into his palm. He winced.

But when Mildred came closer, her face radiated such kindly acceptance that Sawyer immediately knew why people trusted her.

He hoped that Delilah would feel the same way.

"Welcome!" Mildred said. "Please, come in. I'll show you to your rooms and then you'll want to bring in your luggage. You must be Delilah. I'm so happy you're here." She kept up a steady stream of chatter, including the little girl but not focusing on her, so eventually Sawyer felt Delilah's grip loosen and she turned her face up to study the tall woman who strode beside them.

"I apologize for our delay," Sawyer said. He gave a condensed version of their unplanned stop at the veterinary clinic. He chose not to mention that after less than an hour in town he'd already made a rival. That had to be some kind of record.

"Oh, so you met Bridget," Mildred said with satisfaction. "She's such a lovely young woman, so friendly to everyone."

"I'm sure that's true," he murmured and shifted from one foot to another. Mildred's words only made him more puzzled as to Bridget's initial reaction to him, a wariness that was there even before he'd announced that he was considering buying the clinic.

Mildred's curious eyebrows signaled that she wanted more details, but she was interrupted by a red-haired boy streaking by.

"Tyson Belvedere," Mildred scolded gently. "Slow down before you knock our new guests right off their feet. This is Sawyer Blume and his daughter, Delilah. They'll be staying with me for a week or so."

Or maybe longer, Sawyer added silently.

"Sorry!" Tyson showed a gap-toothed grin. "I gotta go. I get to walk home by myself now because I'm eight. Nice to meetcha."

"Tyson's adoptive father, Paul, is married to one of our elementary school teachers," Mildred explained. "Charlotte is Bridget's cousin, as a matter of fact. They legally adopted Tyson last year. Let me tell you, there is quite a story there."

Sawyer was sure that there was and he paused to imagine what it would be like to settle here in Green Valley, to get to know the people, their stories and their histories; for Delilah to make new friends and return to her former confident self, instead of the silent shadow of the girl she used to be.

"Maybe someday I'll get to hear it," he said.

"Tyson was here today because his parents needed to drive into the city for an appointment," Mildred said. "I'm sure he'll want to come back sometime and play with Delilah. You'd like that, wouldn't you, Tyson?"

"Sure," he agreed cheerfully before speeding off.

Delilah studied her pink sneakers and pushed her hair back behind her ears.

Sawyer knew that at some point he would have to offer an explanation for his daughter's reluctance to speak, or at least come up with some version that wasn't unbearable to think about. But now wasn't the time, so he said, "I'll get our luggage. I'd like to help Delilah start to feel settled in before we join you for supper."

"That sounds like a good plan," Mildred agreed. "Please, take your time and do whatever you need to do."

"Thank you. Okay, Delilah, let's get our things."

Mildred showed them to their rooms, but before going to his Sawyer wanted to make sure that Delilah felt safe and comfortable.

The room was small and cozy, with a gleaming hardwood floor, a pink-and-white circular braided rug and a flowered pink quilt on the bed.

"You'll feel right at home here, won't you, Dee-Dee?" Sawyer urged hopefully, but his head pulsed with anxiety. Yes, Delilah always wore something pink these days, but it had been her mother's signature color, not hers. Delilah had been an active, trumpeting-voiced tomboy who favored jeans and earthy colors. She would have been far more likely to have followed him around, mimicking his actions. He understood all too well why she wore pink, but it had nothing to do with her truly liking the color.

How could everything about their life change between one breath and the next? He once again asked himself and God the unanswerable question. When someone went to the store for less than twenty minutes to get snacks for their movie viewing he was supposed to come home and find things as he left them. He was not supposed to find his wife dead on the kitchen floor because the clot that had been making its silent, insidious way through her body had burst and most definitely, their almost-seven-year-old daughter should never ever have been the sole witness.

No, it never should have happened, but it had. And now he was left to try to piece back together a little girl while being perpetually unsure of how long he could hold himself together.

"It's a nice room, isn't it, Dee-Dee?"

Delilah nodded. "Yes, Daddy," she said, her whisper so soft he could hardly hear it.

What he wouldn't give to hear her shout and argue and drop a jelly sandwich facedown on the clean floor. He loved this whispering, pink-clad little girl so much that it consumed him. He loved her but he hardly knew who she was.

He wished that his thoughts wouldn't keep returning to Bridget Connelly and her declaration that she intended to purchase the clinic. He wished that the sadness and vulnerability he sensed lurking behind her determined exterior didn't cause sympathetic stirrings in him.

Along with what he and Delilah were already going through, his father's wishes and expectations were enough to deal with.

There was no doubt that his father's work ethic was stronger than most and, much of the time, Sawyer had admired it and wanted to be like him, in the sense that he wanted to be able to give Tina and Delilah everything they desired. But he had also sensed the loneliness his mother hid behind her constant bustling and organizing, the ideal wife for a hardworking businessman, and he had made himself and Tina a promise that he would be more than a husband who showed up to gulp down supper, too tired and preoccupied for conversation.

He had done his best to keep his promise but it hadn't been enough. It was all too easy for business to get in the way.

In the last few weeks, his mother had started doing something that she had never done before: she urged his father to rest more, to forget about work.

Of course, asking Hank Blume to do that was like asking him to cut off his own hand.

But Sawyer didn't want to think about his family or about his futile past efforts to love and protect his wife and daughter. And, he definitely didn't want to think about what Bridget Connelly's dreams might be.

It would take everything he had to believe in his own.

On Tuesday morning, as with most mornings, Bridget's alarm went off early so that she could use the time before work to study. She sprang out of bed before she could succumb to the temptation to give the snooze button a workout. Lack of sleep was a chronic problem in her life these days, but she needed to make the most of morning time, especially when she had other things going on in the evening such as her support group tonight.

Her nerves fluttered at the thought of sharing at the meeting tonight. She usually looked forward to sharing. The women in the group had welcomed her unconditionally, with warmth and without judgment. They were playing a huge part in her road to recovery and she wanted to do the same for them.

But Sawyer Blume's declaration that he was thinking about buying the clinic was a persistent itch that distracted her from other things. She wished that she wasn't obligated to assist his audit over the next few days.

His little girl, Delilah, was a different story, though. Bridget was struck by Sophie's immediate bond with her and was curious about her whispers and the unchildish sadness that lurked in her eyes. Seeing the positive impact she and Sophie appeared to have on each other gave her all the more reason to believe in her program and what she wanted to accomplish with it.

Chasing these thoughts around meant that she was still unclear about what she would say at the group, but now she had to focus on her homework.

"Come on, Sophie." She coaxed the dog down from the bed, choosing to ignore the fact that she wasn't supposed to be up there in the first place. Sophie followed her to the kitchen, eager for her breakfast.

Bridget's kitchen was white with accents of light blue. It had a fresh, open design and was one of her favorite rooms in her house.

After coffee was made and poured, and she had her usual breakfast selection of a whole wheat bagel, light cream cheese and an assortment of fresh fruit, the only thing that took precedence over her homework was fifteen minutes of devotional time.

But, as she idly turned her Bible's pages to find the scripture for the day's reading, Bridget knew her heart wasn't in it. Church had always been an important part of her family's life and she still believed in God, but she didn't understand why He hadn't protected her from Wes.

She forced herself to read the scripture from Joshua 1:9, which reminded her to be brave and courageous because God was always with her.

She wanted to believe that but it wasn't easy anymore.

Bridget snapped her Bible shut and took her coffee over to her computer, where she was soon absorbed in her studies.

Animals were more complex than people believed. Studies showed that they didn't operate purely by instinct but could be driven by emotion and the need for companionship and could self-sacrifice for their young or for the sake of the greater good. Unlike people, Bridget thought, they were loyal and they loved unconditionally.

I wonder where Delilah's mother is.

Bridget reread the passage she had just read, determined not to get distracted.

There was something about Sawyer and Delilah that struck a chord with her, but there was no way she could let him buy the business, which meant that she had to push her self-doubts aside and make an appointment with the bank. She promised herself to do so as soon as the bank opened.

Sophie whimpered to go outside.

"Sorry about that, Soph." Bridget followed the wagging-tailed dog to the back door and watched her amble around on the lawn for a little while before doing her business.

After she let Sophie back inside, Bridget returned to her homework but the time went too quickly and before she knew it, it was time to get ready for work. She hadn't made as much progress on the assignment as she'd hoped and, with the meeting tonight, it would mean another late night.

But it was important that she continue to attend support group meetings and to work hard toward her goals. There was no way she wanted to slip back to being the person that Wes had convinced her she was…a nobody with nothing to offer.

She was almost out the door when her phone rang.

"Hi, Bridge, I'm glad I caught you," Charlotte Belvedere said.

"You almost didn't," Bridget said. Her heart tugged between love and guilt as it always did these days when she spoke to Charlotte. For the most part, she had been avoiding Charlotte because she didn't want to discuss her breakup with Wes, no matter how well-meaning Charlotte's interest was.

Her support group encouraged her to share, to

open up to her family and trust that the people who loved her and knew her best would understand and be on her side.

"It's not your shame," Mavis always reminded her. "You didn't invite this, want this or deserve this. Wes is the one with the problem, not you."

In some part of her, Bridget understood that, but she just wasn't ready yet.

The family had already had so much sorrow to deal with following the drowning death of Charlotte's little sister many years ago. They had all worked hard to find the joy in life again and the last thing she wanted was to be the person who brought it all crashing down.

"What's up, Char?" Bridget asked. "I was just leaving for work."

"Steph and I are meeting for lunch at Seth's," Charlotte said, referring to Stephanie Winslow, a good friend of theirs who worked in the pharmacy at Dudley's Drugstore. "Seth's" was Seth's Café, owned by Seth Acoose, an energetic, hardworking Indigenous man who thrived on interacting with his customers and serving them the best food in town. His wife, Rena, was a schoolteacher like Charlotte.

"We wondered if you wanted to join us," Charlotte suggested. "I feel like it's been a while since we've really hung out. Seth is getting a complex because you're never at the café anymore," she added teasingly.

Bridget forced a chuckle. She did love Seth's, but she still wasn't up to its bustling atmosphere where everyone knew—or wanted to know— each other's business. Regret mixed with relief as she answered, "I wish I could but I should stick around work today in case the auditor Doc B hired needs my help with anything."

She didn't mention the words they had exchanged over the purchase of the clinic. Her stomach clenched as she thought about calling the bank.

"But we'll definitely do lunch soon," she said.

"I'm holding you to that," Charlotte said.

They said their goodbyes and Bridget clicked off her phone.

Bridget usually liked to arrive at the clinic at least fifteen minutes before they opened so she had time to put on the coffee, check the email and phone messages and prepare herself for the day, and today she also wanted to make that call to the bank.

Dr. Burgess ran on the early side too and Charlotte's phone call had put Bridget slightly behind schedule, so she was surprised to find the closed sign still displayed on the door, and her nerves jangled when she saw Sawyer Blume waiting outside the locked door. Sophie's cautious whine indicated that she wasn't thrilled either.

"You're here early." She gripped Sophie's leash tightly.

"Are you okay?" Sawyer's concerned expression made her aware of the tightness of her face.

"I'm fine," Bridget replied hurriedly. "I'm just surprised to see you here. If you'll excuse me I need to make a call."

"I didn't mean to get here so early," Sawyer explained. "I guess I overestimated how long it would take."

"It's easy to do that if you're used to bigger cities," Bridget said, allowing herself to smile.

She unlocked the door and ushered him in, showing him to a chair in the reception area.

Just what was it about Sawyer that set her so off-balance? It was more than his early arrival. It was even more than the potential purchase of the clinic.

It was something you couldn't pay her to get within a hundred feet of.

Bridget explained that she had a phone call to make and went into a small room in a hallway off the reception area, closing the door behind her.

The bank loans officer Bridget wanted to deal with was away, so she made her appointment for the following Monday. There was almost a whole week to wait. Her bagel set heavily in her stomach at the thought of it, but at least she had taken a step forward.

"I'm probably intruding on your morning routine," Sawyer said, when she came back out to where he sat.

Bridget was surprised to hear him express concern about interrupting her routine. For the first time since they arrived at the clinic, she really looked at him and regretfully registered that he was even better-looking in business attire. But his face was more than just tired. It was weary with dark circles etched under his eyes and tension bracketing his mouth.

"Did you have a bad night?" she asked cautiously. She didn't want to get involved but she couldn't ignore obvious distress, any more than she could turn her back on a child or an animal that needed her.

"Delilah doesn't always adjust well to new surroundings," Sawyer said. "She had nightmares. Mildred got her busy looking at old photos this morning, so I thought I'd better leave while Delilah was reasonably calm."

His sudden involuntary jerk signaled that he was surprised he had said so much.

"Anyway—" he smacked his palms together, all business again "—since we're here we might as well get started."

Bridget unhooked Sophie's leash. The dog cast a suspicious look in Sawyer's direction, before heading to somewhere in the back of the clinic.

"Would you like some coffee?" she asked as she automatically started preparing a pot, not making eye contact with him. She pushed the on button and went into the small staff lounge to get two mugs, all the while aware of Sawyer walking slowly around the office, taking everything in.

The clinic was bright and clean and spacious but now, knowing he was looking at it with the eyes of a potential buyer, she almost wished it wasn't.

Dear God, please, I need to get that loan. These days she didn't know if God was listening, but she wasn't taking any chances.

In the meantime, she still had her job to do.

"This is where you'll be working," Bridget said, showing Sawyer into the office. "I'll just get you signed in."

She sat at the computer and tapped in a password.

"The password is here." She showed Sawyer a sticky note inside the top drawer of the desk. "This is the software you'll be using." She clicked on it and again the computer took an agonizingly long time to open the file, which she was especially conscious of with Sawyer standing over her shoulder.

His aftershave smelled of pine, an enticing scent—something that she did not want to notice.

The file finally clicked open.

Thankfully, Sawyer was familiar with the software so she didn't have to spend time explaining it to him.

But now an awkward silence hung between them.

Sawyer's cell phone played out some Mozart in the midst of the silence, startling both of them.

"Excuse me," he said, and answered it with an anxious expression. "I see…okay. I understand. I—I can come back. I think it's best." He hung up and slid the phone back into his pocket.

"I'm afraid I'll have to go for a little while," he said. "I'm not sure how long. That was Mildred. Delilah has been…" He paused as if trying to find a word that would encompass what had brought the slump to his shoulders and etched the painful weariness more deeply into his face. "Struggling," he concluded.

"Maybe she could come back here with you," Bridget suggested. "She might like to see Sophie again and I know that you and Doc B still need to go over some things." She checked the time. "I'm kind of surprised she isn't here already."

Her boss worked with the attitude that she wasn't retired until she was retired and had continued to keep regular hours at the office, so her current absence was puzzling.

Bridget told herself that she made the offer because it was the polite thing to do, but the truth was that she just couldn't bear to see someone—even someone who could steal her dreams—look as lost as Sawyer Blume did.

Chapter Three

Bridget Connelly was a hard one to figure out.

Yesterday everything about her, from the ice in her blue eyes to her body language, had shown that she considered him to be a huge obstacle. But now sympathy and compassion shone from her face. Her softened expression made him notice how pretty she was, which was probably not a good thing.

Gratitude struggled against more complex feelings.

Please God, he prayed silently. *Help me to know what I should do here.*

As if in answer, Sophie entered from wherever she'd been hiding, gave Sawyer a once-over and wagged her tail slightly, reminding him that what he remembered most about the unsettling experience from yesterday was not his panic but the unexpected sight of his daughter's happy interaction with Sophie and Bridget.

That had to be worth something.

"If you're sure?" he asked Bridget.

"As long as it's okay with Doc B."

At that moment, Dr. Burgess arrived with apologies for running late. "I had to check on my mother," she explained.

"How is she doing?" Bridget asked.

"Not so good," the doctor responded. "She keeps forgetting to take her medication. She's getting so forgetful." She shook her head. But then her caring, efficient manner returned.

"How are things here this morning?" She extended her hand to Sawyer. "You must be Sawyer Blume. Good to officially meet you."

Sawyer shook her hand. "It's nice to meet you too."

He was anxious to check on Delilah but he didn't want Dr. Burgess to think that he didn't take his work seriously.

It was Bridget who stepped in and explained the situation and what seemed to be the obvious solution.

"Not a problem at all," Dr. Burgess said. "Whatever gets the job done."

Sawyer silently thanked God. He couldn't imagine any of his usual clients being so understanding and he recalled what Bridget had said about the people in Green Valley looking out for each other.

"I really appreciate this," he said. "I'll go and see if Delilah will come back with me. This is very kind of you—of both of you." He glanced at Bridget, who was bent over Sophie, scratching her ears.

Still avoiding me, he thought. *One step forward and two steps back.* But why did he care about making any steps forward?

He didn't like the unease that sifted through him at making an offer on the business Bridget had stated she wanted to buy. The only person he needed to focus on was Delilah.

But if Delilah was unhappy here, maybe his best option was to get the job done as quickly as possible and get her back to familiar surroundings. Grief lurked around every corner at home but at least it was a grief they were used to.

"I won't be long," he said.

Sawyer called Mildred back to let her know that he was on his way and what the plan was.

A little while later, he had scarcely set foot back in her yard when the front door burst open and Delilah hurled herself down the steps and toward him. She grabbed both his hands and clung on with all her might.

Sawyer looked down at his daughter, his heart tugging between love and frustration. Delilah wore a T-shirt but still had on her pink pajama bottoms. Her hair wasn't brushed and had a frayed pink ribbon trailing from it. Her face was set in defiance, but a silent plea lurked beneath the stony surface.

Once again he was torn between impossible choices. Maybe he was only being selfish to think Delilah would do better in a different environment. It was hard to keep the fact that he wasn't seeing eye to eye with his father or Marc on business decisions out of the picture.

Mildred followed closely behind, with an apology on her kindly face.

"I'm sorry," she said. "I didn't mean to upset Delilah. I offered to brush her hair and put a new ribbon in it."

Sawyer smoothed his hand over his daughter's hair and met Mildred's eyes above her head.

"No need to apologize," he said. "I know your intentions were good. It's just been a difficult time, but that doesn't excuse Delilah's behavior. Delilah, please apologize to Miss Price."

"I don't think that's necessary," Mildred protested.

"It is necessary," Sawyer said. It was necessary that he didn't allow the upheaval in their lives to stop him from raising the kind of person he wanted Delilah to be.

"Now, please, Delilah," he urged.

"Sorry," she whispered to the ground and

Sawyer felt the rawness of the words in his own throat.

"And I'm sorry too, Delilah," Mildred responded promptly. "Now, let's put it behind us."

As he and his daughter made their way back to the clinic, Sawyer reminded her that he would be working, but would be close by. "Bridget said you could help her with Sophie in the back. Does that sound okay?"

Delilah's answer was a little skip beside him, as she began to hum something by Mozart.

"Your little girl knows something from *The Marriage of Figaro*?" Bridget asked as they entered with Delilah continuing to hum with enthusiasm. "What?" She raised her eyebrows at the startled expression on Sawyer's face. "Do you think you're the only one who knows classical music?"

Bridget kept surprising him, something he couldn't help but admire.

Delilah and Sophie saw each other and the dog's entire body immediately went into a greeting of frenzied joy. Sawyer watched as his daughter went to Sophie, flung her arms around her neck and began to whisper a torrent of words into the dog's ear.

He would give anything to know what she was sharing and he wished there was some way he could know if staying in Green Valley was the right thing to do.

Once he got started, it shouldn't take him more than a week, if even that, to complete the audit. It wasn't nearly enough time to decide whether Green Valley could be a permanent home for them. He didn't know what had prompted him to tell Bridget he was thinking of making an offer on the property. It was probably just a moment of wishful thinking.

But, please, Lord, we need something. Something has to change before we both break apart and can't gather the pieces anymore.

When Sawyer knew that Delilah was contentedly occupied with Sophie, he went into the office that had been assigned to him, started up the computer and waited for the program to load.

He recalled how long this process had taken when Bridget showed it to him, so he wasn't overly concerned about the extended wait. But then, a fatal-error message flashed up on the screen and it went completely black.

He stepped outside the office. "Dr. Burgess? Bridget? We have a problem."

Dr. Burgess came out of her office and Bridget came from somewhere in the back, offering assurance that Delilah was happy brushing Sophie.

"That's great," Sawyer said. "But I think I've just crashed the computer." He removed his glasses and briefly pinched the bridge of his nose before putting them back on again.

"Oh, I'm sure it's not you," Dr. Burgess said. "We've been having trouble with that software ever since we installed it. I would suggest trying another computer but don't want to risk it. Bridget, what do you think?"

Bridget was searching Sawyer's face—for what, he wasn't sure.

Finally, she said, "I think I'd better make some phone calls."

She retreated behind the receptionist's station and Sawyer heard snatches of conversation.

A few minutes later she was back, looking slightly grim. "There's definitely a glitch with the software," she reported. "They have an order in on another kind, which they promise has been tested more extensively. But it won't be in for at least a couple of weeks."

Sawyer's head swarmed with thoughts. Two weeks. Too long to stay in Green Valley with no purpose, but too short a time to go home, raise his father's expectations and get Delilah resettled before another upheaval.

No, there had to be another answer.

"I really apologize for the inconvenience," he said. "I can do the work manually."

"Not your fault," Dr. Burgess said briskly. "Yes, you can do the work manually but there's no real rush, is there? One of the perks of owning my own business in a small town is that I get to decide when things get done. You could do the work manually, or you and your little girl could take some time to get to know our town a little better. Besides, I think you'll do an even better job of assessing the business if you understand how our whole community is knit together."

It echoed what Bridget had said, but when Sawyer glanced her way she kept her head bowed over a note she was writing.

"Bridget would be a great person to show you around," Dr. Burgess suggested.

Bridget's head flew up and her face flushed. "Well…if you think that would be the best use of my time."

"I think that forming bonds is the way we do business here in Green Valley," Dr. Burgess said in a "the matter is settled" voice.

Sawyer was about to excuse Bridget from the obligation when, unexpectedly, his grandmother's voice came into his head and he could almost picture her sitting across from him, her eyes sharp but kind.

God does work in mysterious ways.

Hiding her discomfort, Bridget excused herself to the back room where Delilah was still engaged in brushing Sophie. Watching the smooth and steady strokes of the brush and Sophie's utter bliss helped calm her nerves.

Whatever her tangled thoughts were about this little girl's father and the predicament she found herself in, Bridget promised herself that she would be a friend and a helper to Delilah as long as she could be.

She'd concluded that Delilah didn't have a cold but was choosing, for whatever reason, to use her voice minimally. It tweaked her curiosity but more than that, the little girl struck a chord in her that she tried to keep buried since she had exposed her hopes and dreams to Wes and he had maliciously smashed each one.

It was hard to believe that only a couple of years ago, when Charlotte met Paul and was involved in her volunteer work with missions at the church, she—Bridget—cared about her job, adored her family and community, but, most of all, she wanted to meet that one special man who would give her the home and family she longed for. Life had seemed full of possibilities.

Not anymore.

Shaking aside the regret that crept through her, Bridget said, "You're doing a great job." She gently stroked her hand over the little girl's tangled hair.

Please, Lord, be with this little girl, Bridget

prayed. *Let her feel Your presence. Whatever she and her dad have been through, they need You.*

The little girl's gentle grooming coaxed a happy whine from Sophie and Delilah giggled.

"Do you have any pets?" Bridget asked.

Delilah shook her head.

"Well, you're great with Sophie." It did Bridget's heart good to see the slow, shy smile that spread across Delilah's face.

"Would you like to give Sophie a treat?" Bridget asked.

Delilah nodded eagerly.

"But you can't just let her grab it," Bridget cautioned. "She has to use her manners." She demonstrated, coaxing Sophie to sit and then urging her to be gentle as she accepted the dog biscuit. "Now you try." She handed another biscuit to Delilah.

The dog was taut with anticipation but she managed to hold her pose until the little girl rewarded her. Bridget smiled at the look of pride on their faces.

This was a perfect example of why the program she hoped to administer meant so much to her. She could think of so many ways it could benefit both humans and animals who had experienced trauma. This was only the second time that Delilah and Sophie had met, yet she could already see the difference they made to one another. The key was trust, not an easy thing to build, or to rebuild once it was shattered.

No doubt there was a lesson that could be learned from Sophie's willingness to risk trusting some people again, even though her former owners had abandoned her. Unfortunately, regular meals, a roof over her head, even gentle voices weren't quite enough to soothe away Bridget's emotional scars.

Bridget heard Dr. Burgess's phone ring and a moment later Sawyer popped his head into the room. Sophie slunk under the examination table and Delilah dropped to her knees and crawled after her.

My feelings exactly, Bridget thought.

She knew that she couldn't judge every man by Wes, but knowing it and *living* it were two very different things. It was still difficult for her to trust her own perceptions.

Since she'd been attending meetings of the abuse support group, she realized how common that was, how abusers were master manipulators, casting blame and pointing fingers, twisting things until their victims didn't know what to think or believe anymore. There was some comfort in knowing that she wasn't alone in that regard, but it was a small, unsatisfying comfort, like a spoonful of lukewarm soup.

"Dr. Burgess had to take a call," Sawyer said. "How's it going in here?"

"It's great," Bridget said. "Well, it was. Please pay no attention to the dog and little girl under the table," she intoned, quelling her nerves with a joke. "There's nothing to see here."

"Hmm, don't think I'll take your word for it," Sawyer said. He bent over and peered at Delilah and Sophie.

"It's okay," Delilah whispered, stroking Sophie's head. "It's my dad. He's nice."

Sophie's sideways look was skeptical but she sighed and rested her head on her paws.

Was he nice, Bridget wondered? It was a simple word but one she wasn't sure she would ever trust again.

"I guess it won't hurt her to sit under there for a few more minutes," Sawyer said, as if he was trying to convince himself.

"I guess not," Bridget said, then added, "I promise it's clean down there."

Silence pulsed between them and Bridget couldn't stand her curiosity any longer.

"Delilah's mother?" she asked tentatively. "Are you...?"

"She passed away." His terseness told her that further questions were unwelcome.

"I'm so sorry," Bridget said.

He nodded. There was a tangible silence under the table.

Bridget changed the subject. "So, how does a music lover end up doing audits?"

Sawyer's expression showed that he knew what she'd done and why, and was grateful for it.

"It's part of the family business," he said. "I guess deep down I always knew I'd join it. It's what my parents expected and it's the practical choice, especially now."

Once again, Bridget felt like it was himself he was trying to convince. Maybe they had that in common. For a long time, she tried to believe that if she kept telling herself—and everyone else—that things were fine it would mean that they were.

"Delilah likes music too," she noted. "You know, once a month we have music nights at the church I attend. Maybe you'd like to bring her to one."

What am I doing?

"That might be fun," Sawyer said. "Listen, I know Dr. Burgess put you on the spot with that whole town tour thing."

"No," Bridget said slowly, as something dawned on her. "I think Doc B is right. It wouldn't hurt for you to get to know our community a little better."

And maybe God would help him understand how much this community meant to her and why she needed the clinic so badly for the work she felt called to do.

She wondered about Sawyer's faith and if he'd managed to sustain it after his wife's death, or if he was struggling like she struggled with her own faith.

Out in the office, Dr. Burgess's phone conversation continued.

"What about you?" Sawyer asked. "Did you always know you wanted to work with animals?"

"I did," Bridget confirmed. "I have plans for this place that I'm not prepared to give up on." Her stomach somersaulted and she swallowed as she thought of her upcoming meeting at the bank.

"I understand," Sawyer said. "I really do. I'm just looking for the best way to help my daughter."

Their words hung between them like an opaque curtain. Then Sawyer leaned down to look under the table. "Delilah, it's time to come out from there."

Delilah crawled out but Sophie remained where she was, exuding a mournful huff that her new best friend had abandoned her.

Dr. Burgess's phone call finally ended and she came out of her office, explaining that there'd been an incident with her mother at the care home where she lived.

"I hope things are okay now," Bridget said.

"Yes, they're fine—for now." Dr. Burgess looked troubled. "It's getting harder to juggle things, though. I really do need to find a buyer for this clinic sooner rather than later."

Panic shot through Bridget and Sawyer avoided making eye contact with her.

Bridget resolved then that she would do her job and be civil with Sawyer. She would make sure that his daughter felt welcome.

But she wouldn't let herself forget, not for one second, that Sawyer was her rival and that they both had an eye on the same property.

No matter how appealing his obvious love for his daughter made him.

Chapter Four

On Thursday morning, Sawyer and Bridget sat in Dr. Burgess's office. With all that was going on, Bridget was glad to have her presentation to the support group over with. Despite her nervousness, it had gone well. The group was always so understanding and supportive. Dr. Burgess tapped a finger on her chin, thoughtfully, and then folded her hands on her desk.

Sawyer exchanged an uncomfortable glance with Bridget.

"I'm afraid I'm going to have to take some time away from the clinic," Dr. Burgess said. "As I've mentioned, my mother has been having some difficulties and I need to focus on that, not be trying to divide my time between wrapping things up here and attending to my mother."

"That's perfectly understandable," Bridget said.

They were the right words but Sawyer could hear wariness in her voice.

"I've asked Dr. Davidson to take over for me," the doctor continued, naming an associate of hers who worked in a nearby farming community. "I wish I could give you a time frame, but I'm not sure at the moment. Sawyer—" she turned her focus to him "—we're already dealing with computer issues and this could slow things down even more. I would fully understand if you wanted to reschedule things and take your little girl back home until I'm back and everything's in place."

Bridget sat up straighter, waiting for his reply.

Maybe a day ago, Sawyer might have considered that the best option was to go back home. But that morning he had left Delilah contentedly shelling peas for their supper with Mildred and the peaceful scene had given him hope. He also couldn't discount the way she was around Sophie...and Bridget. Even seeing small, fleeting glimmers of her previous happiness and confidence was far better than being at home, where she could curl into the shell of dark memory again.

"I'm fine with staying," he answered. "Delilah seems to be enjoying herself here and I'm sure we can find ways to keep ourselves busy."

Telling his family that he would be delayed wasn't going to be easy, but he would deal with that later. Perhaps it could be the precursor to telling them he was done with the family business for good. The thought of making an offer on the clinic was still a tantalizing one, even if there was a lot to consider first.

Right now his heart was at peace with the decision and he intended to hang on to that as long as he could.

"How does this impact me?" Bridget spoke up. Her tone was respectful but there was a thin-blade edge to it when she added, "Should I be spending my time as Sawyer's tour guide, or should I be doing other things?"

Dr. Burgess looked between them, and Sawyer had the oddest feeling that behind her professionally calm demeanor she wanted to smile.

"I will still need you at the clinic every day, of course," she said. "People may phone for appointments and Dr. Davidson will need your assistance for whatever business we do get. I don't have any problems with you doing homework as time allows."

"But you still want me to play host to Sawyer?" Bridget asked flatly.

"I would appreciate it, yes."

Sheer curiosity kept Sawyer from insisting again that a tour guide wasn't necessary. He couldn't help wanting to know more about Bridget: what kind of person she was—or had been. Something lurked behind her pretty face that spoke of loss, a language he understood all too well.

On Friday morning, before going down for breakfast, Sawyer decided not to put off calling home any longer, but couldn't help his relief when it was his mother who answered.

"Sawyer, I was just thinking of you. How soon will you be home?"

He removed his glasses as tension began to thread its way into his head and neck.

Being as succinct as possible, he explained the delays and his decision to remain in Green Valley for the interim.

"I really wish you would reconsider that choice, Sawyer," his mother said. Her way of speaking was rarely anything other than well modulated and controlled, but he could almost see her tight grip on the phone. "Your father needs you."

"I'm sure Dad and Marc can run the business without me for a little while longer," Sawyer said. He knew his mother considered it proper to take her husband's side, but some encouragement and support from his mother would have been welcome.

There was silence on the end of the phone for a moment, then she said, "Well, there's not much more I can tell you, but I'm sure your father will be getting in touch with you after I tell him you called."

"Yes, I'm sure he will."

After a pause his mother asked, "How is Delilah? Doesn't she want to come home?"

"Delilah's fine," he said. "Actually, she really seems to like it here." He told his mother about Sophie but for some reason he didn't want to tell her about Bridget.

Was that because his unbidden interest in her confused him or because he didn't want his family to think that he'd forgotten about Tina?

Whatever the reason, he was disgruntled by the time the call was over.

In Mildred's kitchen he was comforted by the smells of carrot-pineapple muffins and freshly brewed coffee that permeated the air. Delilah sat in the chair across from him and put her feet up on his so he could tie her pink shoelaces. He was relieved that it was her only touch of pink today, choosing to see it as some progress—however small—that she was inching her way back to being her old self.

"Now, do you remember what we talked about?" he asked her.

Delilah nodded.

"So we agree that if you have a nice morning with Mildred, then I can ask Ms. Connelly if you can come and see Sophie in the afternoon. Is that a deal?"

She solemnly extended her hand, indicating

that they should shake on it. Her hand felt small and fragile in his and Sawyer swallowed before giving it a firm shake.

Mildred came over to the table and set a plate of warm muffins between them. Her white braids were wrapped around her head and her flowery ruffled apron was incongruous with her denim overalls. She sat down and cut a muffin in half, buttered it and put one half on Delilah's plate.

"We are going to be just fine, aren't we?" the older woman said with cheerful confidence. "Delilah, would you mind getting some more orange juice out of the fridge?"

The little girl slid down off her chair and Mildred used the opportunity to say quietly. "It *will* be fine, Sawyer." He got the feeling she was talking about more than just that particular morning.

He had told her about the unexpected delays and she had assured him that they were welcome to stay at her house for as long as they needed to. She appeared, in fact, to be quite happy about the new developments.

Delilah headed back to the table, clutching the orange juice carton carefully with both hands, and set it down on the table.

"Lovely, thank you," Mildred said.

Delilah nodded. Then her eyes went to Mildred's crown of braids and she touched her tangled hair.

"Would you like me to braid your hair?" Mildred asked.

Delilah nodded again.

"Can you answer Miss Price, please?" Sawyer encouraged.

"Yes, please," Delilah whispered.

"I'd love to," Mildred said. "When you're finished your muffin and juice, you can go upstairs to the bathroom and in the top drawer on the right you'll find a hairbrush and some elastics and ribbons."

Delilah finished eating hurriedly and pushed back her chair.

"I'm going to be leaving soon," Sawyer said, preparing her. Bridget had asked him to meet her at Seth's Café. The animal clinic didn't open until 10:00 a.m. on Fridays and she said that if he was serious about getting to know Green Valley the café was a great place to start.

"Okay, Daddy." She hugged him and then set off to find the hair supplies.

"I told you things would be okay." Mildred's eyes twinkled. "Tyson—the little red-haired boy you met when you first got here—is coming over to play."

"That sounds good," Sawyer said, remembering a little girl with a troop of friends constantly stomping in and out of their house, her voice and laughter ringing out louder than anyone else's. But that little girl was gone and he didn't know if she would ever come back.

Delilah returned with a hairbrush in one hand and a handful of ribbons and elastics in the other.

"Good job," Mildred praised her. "If you want to take them into the living room, I'll be right there."

"Tyson is a very nice little boy," Mildred assured him when Delilah departed. "His parents died in an accident so he's someone who can understand what Delilah is going through."

"Maybe," Sawyer said.

"You sound skeptical," Mildred said, not unkindly.

"I think that grief is complicated," Sawyer answered, after a pause. "We all grieve in our own ways."

And how he was supposed to grieve was something he was still trying to figure out. Being brutally shoved into a single-parent role to a troubled daughter hadn't left him with a whole lot of time to sort out his own feelings. He read scriptures about how God comforted people in their sorrow but struggled to apply those promises to his own life.

"I'm glad to hear you're meeting up with

Bridget," Mildred said, changing the subject, for which Sawyer was grateful. That was until she added, "She's a lovely woman and would make a good friend for you."

"Dr. Burgess asked her to show me around," he said. "It's nothing more than that."

"Well, maybe it could be," Mildred suggested. "I think you could both use a friend."

Sawyer thought it was an odd thing to say about someone who'd lived in Green Valley her whole life and would surely have plenty of friends, but he didn't say so.

"Thank you for everything," he said instead. He checked the time and added, "I'd better get going."

"Give my best to Bridget," Mildred said brightly. "Maybe after breakfast, you could ask her to show you where the library and museum are. I think you and Delilah would enjoy visiting them sometime."

Sawyer nodded, tucking in a rueful smile. Mildred was nothing if not persistent.

As Sawyer walked to the café, he took in the unique Main Street shops—no box stores or chain restaurants to be seen. People he didn't know nodded and smiled at him, some said, "Good morning," and he responded in kind. At home, he was usually in his car, focused on getting to his next meeting.

Home. His mother's insistence that his father needed him still plagued, as did his guilt that he was still avoiding his father's calls.

He allowed himself to savor the thought of starting over here in this place where people didn't know him when he was married and didn't see him in terms of what he had lost.

Bridget arrived at Seth's Café before her designated meeting time with Sawyer. Knowing how busy things always were at the popular café, she had wanted to be sure she secured a good table.

She also needed a few minutes to prepare herself, not only to spend time with Sawyer, but to face the well-intentioned but curious members of the community who wondered why she hadn't been around.

Wes had not been a fan of Seth's Café. He said it was too crowded, the food was unsophisticated and he didn't like the way people were always coming up to say hi, interrupting their dinner. In short, all the things that Bridget loved about being there.

But she'd also been flattered at first when he insisted on taking her to out-of-the-way, expensive restaurants, located in larger towns in the surrounding area, sitting in dark corners so that they could focus only on the food and each other. Now she realized it had just been another way for him to control her.

"Bridge!"

Bridget looked up to see Charlotte beaming at her. Her cousin had always had a quiet beauty, brought to life by her extraordinary violet eyes. But since she'd married Paul Belvedere, her happiness made her radiant.

She was happy for Charlotte, but sometimes that joy dimmed as she contrasted it to her remorse over her own bad choices.

She smiled up at her cousin, hoping nothing of what she'd been thinking showed on her face.

"It's so great to see you," Charlotte said, giving Bridget's shoulder a gentle squeeze. "I'm here with Paul and Ty. Why don't you come join us?"

"I would," Bridget said, "but I'm meeting Sawyer. He's doing the audit at the clinic," she hurried to explain before Charlotte could get the wrong impression. "But things have been delayed." She briefly recounted the computer problems and Dr. Burgess's decision to take time to focus on her mother. "And she thinks it would be a good idea for me to show him around town," she concluded.

"What's he like?" Charlotte asked.

Bridget was saved from trying to articulate her unsettling reaction to Sawyer because Seth, holding a coffeepot in one hand and menus in the other, escorted him to the table.

"I see you've met Seth," Bridget said, shutting out the thought of how appealing Sawyer looked in his navy blue T-shirt and blue jeans. "And this is my cousin Charlotte Belvedere."

"It's nice to meet you." Charlotte shook his hand. "I was just telling Bridget that you're more than welcome to join my husband and son and me."

Sawyer looked to Bridget and she rapidly weighed out the pros and cons, then remembered that she wanted Sawyer to know her—to know the community and the people who cared about her, so that he would think twice about interfering with her chances to make an offer on the clinic.

As she accepted Charlotte's invitation, she reminded herself that there was nothing personal about the choice, no matter how strangely couple-ish it felt to share a table with a happily married couple.

On Monday morning, Bridget's stomach knotted as she tried to decide what to wear to the bank for her meeting regarding the loan. As if sensing her mood, Sophie was subdued, lying by her feet instead of whining for a game of fetch.

It didn't help matters that she'd received a call from the bank on Friday afternoon to say that the person she'd been counting on meeting with was delayed in returning, but if she wanted to keep her appointment they were sure they could fit her into another loan officer's schedule, whoever happened to have an opening when she arrived.

She wasn't particularly happy about meeting with someone she didn't know well, but she didn't want to postpone things any longer. As far as she knew, Sawyer hadn't made an offer yet, but she was sure he was only waiting until Doc B returned, so she had to make sure her own plan was in place sooner rather than later.

Sawyer... She still didn't know quite what to think about him and she didn't want to be thinking of him at all. The fact that he had been so friendly and polite with Charlotte, Paul and Tyson, showing genuine interest in them and the town, somehow unnerved her even more.

The last thing she wanted was to find him appealing.

She checked the time and quickly chose a flowered dress with a peach, light-knit cardigan to wear over it and silently prayed as she got dressed.

She really needed God to come through for her on this one.

"Be back in a bit." She gave Sophie's ears a distracted scratch and the dog huffed and lowered her head back onto her paws, clearly knowing she wasn't the first priority that morning.

"I'm sorry, Soph. I'm just a little stressed."

Sophie made an empathetic noise in her throat.

Although Bridget was at the bank early, there were already quite a few people there. She waved at Belle Lawrence, who had helped her open her first checking account when she was a thirteen-year-old and earning money as a babysitter, and Belle's smile reassured her.

This was her town and these were people who had known her all her life. They would want to support her and do what they could to help her succeed.

She took a seat in the reception area—her fingers made tight claws around the edge of her purse—and said "No, thank you" to the offer of coffee. Her jittery nerves didn't need caffeine.

"Good morning. Bridget?"

Bridget looked up and didn't recognize the middle-aged man who stood before her, wearing a suit and a professional smile.

"Yes." She started to rise, uncertainly.

"I'm Byron Swift. I understand we'll be meeting this morning." He extended his hand.

Bridget shook it. "I don't think I've ever seen you here," she said.

"Probably not," Byron said. "I was just transferred here at the beginning of the month from Prince Albert and I'm still spending my weekends there, trying to sell my condo and get some other business wrapped up."

Bridget tried to ignore the sinking feeling that accompanied her as she followed Byron into his office, where the lack of personal items reflected his businesslike demeanor.

He didn't know her or what the town and clinic meant to her. But she was here now and would do her best.

You'll never get it. You have nothing to offer.

Bridget bit her lip to stifle the cry that wanted to escape. She could hear Wes's snide voice as clearly as if he were standing right beside her.

Please, Lord. Please help me not to give in to self-doubt.

She took a few deep breaths and prepared herself. Her voice shook when she began speaking but Byron started taking notes and didn't appear to notice. Maybe he expected that people would be nervous when they came in to ask for a loan. Some hope returned as she spoke, but Byron just continued to take notes and his face remained disconcertingly inexpressive.

When she was done speaking, Byron set down his pen, folded his hands on top of his desk and studied her.

"So, you don't actually have your degree yet?"

"No," Bridget said. "But I'm making steady progress toward it while still being employed full-time and I'm doing well in my classes."

Byron retrieved his pen and made another note. "You don't appear to have much of a credit rating."

"I don't use credit cards. I prefer not to buy things unless I can pay up front."

Surely a responsible attitude like that should impress the bank, but Byron was frowning slightly.

"I pay all my bills on time," she added, a little desperately. "And I would do the same with loan payments."

"I'm sure you would," Byron said.

"I wouldn't be asking for a loan if there was any way I could manage the down payment on my own," Bridget said, trying the straightforward approach.

"Well, that's why people ask for loans, right?" Byron smiled. "It's because they don't have the money to do what they want to do."

The smile disappeared and he studied her again. "Have you thought about building your own savings? To be honest, your savings seem to be a bit lacking, but I could give you some tips to rectify that."

The sinking feeling returned and slithered across her stomach.

"I do save as much as I can, after bills and all. My online classes are expensive and I didn't rely on a loan to pay for those. But I need to make a move on this quickly. I don't have the time it would take to save enough money to make a down payment."

"I'm sorry, Bridget," Byron said. "But I have to say I'm not prepared to give you this loan. Your idea sounds good in theory, but you need a more solid business plan. I need more evidence that this is something that could work and that you are the right person to make it work. I just don't believe you have the collateral to make this loan a good risk for the bank, no matter how good your intentions are."

"You don't know me," Bridget said. Her voice rose and Byron's eyebrows rose too. She gripped her purse tightly. "I'm sorry, but I'm sure if you just talked to some of the staff here—Belle Lawrence has known me my whole life…"

"I'm sure that everyone here has a high opinion of you," Byron said. "But the bank hired me as a loans officer because they trust me to make sound decisions, which is what I'm doing here. It's not personal, Bridget, it's just business. Maybe we can talk again in a few months."

He stood up and extended his hand. Bridget's manners kicked in enough for her to shake it briefly, but her head was spinning.

"The property could be gone by then," she said.

"I'm sure that other opportunities will come along and we can revisit things when they do," Byron said. "In the meantime, I strongly recommend you finish up that degree as quickly as you can and get a solid business plan in place."

With those words, Bridget understood that she was being dismissed. She'd had her chance and she'd blown it. Maybe Wes was right.

But she knew that the women in her support group wouldn't want her to give in to those thoughts. They would encourage her to fight whatever power Wes still had over her with every ounce of her being.

It was easy too to think that God had failed to answer her prayers but, frankly, she was tired of giving in to that belief too. Maybe God wasn't assuring her an easy road, but then again, He didn't promise that to anyone. That didn't mean that she should quit, nor did it mean that she couldn't reach out for support when she needed it. The support group meeting wasn't until tomorrow night, but she could reach out and call any of them at any time. That was a promise they made to each other.

There were still so many unanswered questions, though. How was she going to make an offer on the property now? And what was stopping Sawyer from making an offer of his own?

Chapter Five

Sawyer came out of his office when he heard Bridget arrive and saw that her face was drawn and her eyes echoed the headache that he'd been carrying since a conversation with his father that morning. His father had almost worn him down with talk of family loyalty and he was only fortified to stand firm on his decision by the sight of Delilah at the kitchen table, peacefully flipping pages in a picture book about dogs that Mildred had found for her.

"Is everything okay?" he asked. Bridget had only told him that she had an appointment that morning.

He could see her assessing his question, almost visibly drawing into herself, still obviously considering him an opponent, even though they'd enjoyed breakfast with Charlotte and Paul and Tyson a few days ago.

Well, he supposed he couldn't blame her for that but he realized that he wanted her to trust him, or at least not to distrust him.

He just didn't know why, except that he still hadn't forgiven himself for not being there when Tina died. It didn't matter that it was sudden and that no one could have predicted it. It didn't matter that the Bible told him that he was forgiven.

None of it helped him forgive himself.

"It's fine," Bridget said.

He didn't believe her but he didn't know her well enough to push the matter.

"Is Dr. Davidson in?" Bridget asked him as she retrieved messages from the phone.

"Yes."

"Fran wants to bring her cat in again," she remarked, making a note.

Then she put the pen down and sat down abruptly. Her mouth wobbled a bit before she captured it into a firm line.

"You're not okay," Sawyer couldn't help saying, even as he knew it was none of his business.

She raised her head and looked at him, her eyes pools of disappointment.

"I had a bit of setback this morning," she said. "The bank turned down my request for a loan, but I'll figure something out."

"If there's anything I can help with..."

Bridget looked at him like he was speaking

an alien language and he realized how ludicrous it must sound to her: him offering his help when they were both after the same thing.

But her blue eyes spoke of the struggle between fight and surrender in a way that he recognized and couldn't ignore. He did admire her perseverance—her "gumption," his grandmother would have said—and wished there was a way for them to both get what they wanted.

However, if life had taught him anything it was that things were not always—or ever—fair. Things could change in a split second and you had to do whatever you could to protect what remained.

"Get you a coffee?" he amended. "Or tea?"

"Thank you." Bridget looked surprised. "Tea would be nice. There's a box of peppermint tea in the cupboard above the sink in the kitchen. I don't take anything in it."

Sawyer tapped on Dr. Davidson's door to see if he wanted anything from the kitchen.

"No, thanks," the doctor said.

When Sawyer returned with Bridget's tea and a coffee for himself, her expression was a peculiar mixture of pleasure and disbelief.

"What?" he asked.

"Nothing." She shook her head and accepted the tea from him. "Thank you."

She set it down and turned back to him. "I

guess I'm just not used to a man who would do that for me."

"Really? I used to get tea for my wife all the time."

The sadness he expected washed over him. But it wasn't just about Tina. Now it was also in wondering why a lovely woman like Bridget had to be surprised by a gesture of kindness.

His shoulders tightened. He couldn't afford to ask that question.

A woman arrived lugging a cage that looked like it was meant for a small dog, and took out the largest white cat Sawyer had ever seen.

Fran Hudson was a tall and slightly plump woman who appeared to be in her early fifties. She was stylishly dressed in a deep purple pant-suit and wore eyeshadow to match. Her hair, graying with blond highlights, framed her face in a flattering way.

Bridget introduced them to each other and they exchanged greetings, but it was clear that Fran had more pressing things on her mind.

"Oh, Bridget," she said breathlessly, "I really need your expertise now that you're taking those classes. I know the doctors can deal with Mr. Snow's physical ailments but I know that you can get to the heart of what's really bothering him. He's been so lethargic lately. He used to have such a dynamic personality."

The cat hung from her arms like a sack of potatoes, his amber eyes forlorn, and Sawyer stifled a laugh.

"Fran, you need to stop overfeeding him," Bridget said gently but firmly. "I promise that if he loses a few pounds, he'll feel a lot better and start being more active again."

"Oh, I'm sure it's more than that," Fran protested. "Just look at the poor dear."

"Please, give it a try," Bridget urged. "If it doesn't help we can look for other causes. You know we want the best for Mr. Snow, just like you do."

She laid a reassuring hand on Fran's arm and Sawyer was touched by Bridget's firm but kind manner. It was obvious she truly cared about the clients and no doubt could put this property to good use.

But as much as he was beginning to admire her he couldn't let that influence what he needed to do for his daughter and himself. His family's persistent refrain that he needed to come home was making it hard enough to make a decision.

After lunch, Bridget said she wanted to stretch her legs and accompanied him on his walk to pick up Delilah for her time with Sophie.

"You were very good with Fran and her cat," Sawyer said.

"It's because I've known them for so many years." Bridget stopped walking and turned to look at him. "What would you do with the property?"

"Open my own investment firm," Sawyer said.

"Sounds like you're out to turn a profit."

It was a loaded comment and he wasn't going to get into his family dynamics or into the true reason why he was desperate for a change. He didn't owe her any kind of explanation.

They arrived at Mildred's in uncomfortable silence.

Delilah was perched expectantly on the arm of a chair near the entryway. Sawyer's heart flooded with affection. Her face looked freshly scrubbed and her hair was pulled back into a complicated loop of braids.

"You look beautiful, Dee-Dee," he said, scooping her up into a hug. Her thin legs kicked in the air and she smiled bashfully. Then, wanting to smooth things over, he made an aside to Bridget. "I sure hope she isn't expecting me to do this style."

Bridget smiled.

"The braids are easier than they look," Mildred said, coming to the front door as she wiped her hands on her apron. "Bridget is good at hairstyles."

"I like doing hair," Bridget agreed, while Delilah studied her, possibly wondering how her straight hair could emulate the soft waves that cascaded around Bridget's shoulders.

"So you had a good morning?" Sawyer asked, changing the subject because Bridget's silky-looking hair wasn't something he dared to dwell on.

"We did indeed. Delilah was a great help in the kitchen. We made chocolate chip cookies. Tyson helped too. Well—" her eyes twinkled "—in a manner of speaking. He told us he was the official taste tester."

"Did you have fun with Tyson?" Sawyer asked Delilah, setting her down again.

Delilah nodded.

"Go get your shoes, please," Sawyer told her. "Sophie is waiting to see you."

Delilah happily scampered off and he asked Mildred, "Was Tyson okay with— I mean, Delilah doesn't say much."

"Tyson likes to chatter," Mildred said placidly, "and everyone loves a good listener. They did just fine."

Sawyer was relieved but it was tinged with the perpetual sadness that plagued him.

I still feel like no one knows the real Delilah. Will I ever get her back?

On their way to get Sophie, Delilah suddenly

reached out and grabbed his hand, then grabbed Bridget's and bounced between them. A shock of familiarity ran through him, one that was out of context with someone he barely knew. Bridget's expression showed that she was just as uncomfortable, but they couldn't yank their hands away from Delilah when she'd made such a trusting gesture.

"Here we are," Bridget said when they arrived at the animal clinic, the relief in her voice unmistakable. "Just wait here while I get Sophie."

As soon as Sophie saw Delilah she ran straight for the little girl. Delilah made little hops in a circle and Sophie gave a yipping bark to accompany each jump.

"Sophie, you're making me look bad," Bridget complained.

Seeing her flustered with her pink cheeks sent an uncanny rush of protectiveness through Sawyer.

He quickly turned his attention to Delilah, who was whispering a stream of words into Sophie's ear. He would have given anything to know what she was saying.

He prayed that one day his little girl would once again share her secrets with him.

Back at the clinic, Delilah was busy trying to teach Sophie how to shake a paw, Sawyer had gone back into his office and Bridget was attempting to concentrate on her own files when the phone rang.

"Good afternoon, Green Valley Animal Clinic," she answered.

"Bridget, it's Dr. Burgess. I just wanted to check in. How are things going? Any word on the software?"

"Not yet," Bridget said. "But Sawyer has been going over files and accumulating information. He says it won't take long to input things and pull everything together once the computer is up and running again. Fran was here earlier with Mr. Snow," she added. "She thinks he's lost his dynamic personality."

"Which means she's still overfeeding him," Dr. Burgess said.

They chuckled together but Bridget's amusement was shadowed by a cloud. She would miss working with this doctor who knew her and the town so well. And, she still had no real idea what the future held for her.

"How are you and Sawyer getting along?" Dr. Burgess asked.

"It's fine. He's a nice guy."

It was true, so why did she feel like she was dancing around a minefield?

"Delilah is visiting with Sophie right now," she added. "They have a good bond."

"Sounds like they're good for each other," Dr. Burgess said.

"Doc B?" Bridget so wanted to tell her boss about her wish to make an offer on the clinic but after having her loan request turned down, there was no point in raising it, at least not until she had something else figured out.

"Yes?"

"How is your mother?" Bridget asked instead.

"That's actually one of the main reasons I'm calling," the doctor said. "I'm afraid things aren't good. She needs to be moved to a higher-level care unit."

"Oh, I'm sorry to hear that."

"I didn't want to do this over the phone, Bridget, but since we're talking, I might as well say it. I don't think I'll be back to work. I'll come in to finalize business with the audit and wrap things up and, of course, I'll contact all of our clients. But I know now that it's best to start my retirement as soon as possible, so I will be putting the clinic up for sale, sooner rather than later."

Bridget swallowed, unable to find her voice. The reality hit that it wasn't just Sawyer she was competing against but anyone else who could afford to make an offer.

"I won't leave you in the lurch, Bridget," her boss continued. "I'll give you the highest possible references and I want you to keep me posted on your studies."

After they hung up, Bridget tried to work but her thoughts were troubled.

A small tug at her sleeve startled her. She hadn't realized Delilah was beside her.

Delilah patted her side to encourage Sophie to run over to her. "Shake a paw," she whispered. Sophie lifted a paw to her extended hand.

"Excellent," Bridget praised.

"Can I show my daddy?" Delilah whispered.

"Absolutely. I'm sure he'd love to see it."

Bridget watched Sawyer watching Delilah demonstrate the trick. His expression was proud but thoughtful.

It didn't feel right to hope that he didn't get what he wanted so that she could get what she wanted.

She had lost an immeasurable part of herself letting Wes's selfishness dominate her life and she still didn't know when or if she would completely move past it. But maybe a big part of that was being the kind of person she wanted to be and not someone who was driven by the fear of losing out.

Delilah and Sophie demonstrated their trick again and, as he grinned boyishly, the stress and fatigue washed away from his face, at least for the time being.

It made him even more attractive.

Was there any possible way for them to both get what they wanted? She did not want them to be unhappy, at least for Delilah's sake.

She would keep telling herself that's all it was.

Surely there must be other properties, Bridget's thoughts churned. If what Sawyer wanted was to set up an investment firm, it wouldn't have to be this location. But even if she could suggest a different location she still wouldn't be able to make an offer, at least not yet, for this one.

Lord, there must be an answer. Please help me find it.

She mustered every ounce of her inner strength not to buckle under the fear that she would fail. That was the old Bridget, the one who had been under Wes's thumb. She had made too many strides forward to go back.

I will get through this. With Your help, Lord, I will.

After supper and taking Sophie for a short walk, Bridget phoned Mavis, who now had her real estate license after becoming interested in the field when she was first looking for a place for her and her son to live in Green Valley.

"Bridget? What is it?"

It had taken Bridget some time to get used to Mavis's brisk, to-the-point manner, but she understood now that it came from a place of having to protect herself and her son for so many years and she knew that Mavis had a giving heart.

She briefly outlined everything for Mavis: Sawyer's declaration that he might want to make an offer on the clinic, the bank loan not being approved, even Delilah's whispers and her uncanny bond with Sophie.

"I refuse to give up on what I want," Bridget concluded, knowing that Mavis would understand why, on so many levels, it was important to her. "But—I don't know—I just don't think I could be happy achieving my own dreams if it meant squashing someone else's."

"Sounds like you care about them," Mavis said.

A vision of Sawyer's face, how it lit up when he smiled, came to her. But she didn't care about him—not in that way—she couldn't.

"I just think that they've been through a lot," she said carefully. "Sawyer's wife died."

"Huh," Mavis said, thoughtfully. "Not good. But I'm guessing you didn't call just to give me their story. How can I help?"

"I need to know what other business properties are for sale," Bridget said. "I'm hoping that I can point Sawyer in another direction."

"And if you can't?" Mavis asked in her blunt

way. "Plus, where are you going to come up with the money, even if you can convince Sawyer not to offer on the clinic?"

Bridget knew that Mavis wasn't trying to discourage her; it was just her nature to focus on the reality of the situation. But sometimes reality wasn't good enough; sometimes a person had to reach out in faith.

"I'll cross those bridges when I need to," Bridget said. "'One step at a time,'" she quoted one of their meetings' constant reminders.

"Sounds about right," Mavis said. "I'll get you a list of properties."

Bridget thanked her, and after she hung up she prayed again and asked God to add His strength to her purpose.

Mavis's remark that she must care about them drifted in and out of her mind for the remainder of the evening. Maybe, despite everything, she hadn't completely shut down. She was still someone capable of caring for others.

She wasn't ready to consider it being any more than that.

Chapter Six

Sawyer was puzzled about why Bridget had asked Delilah and him to meet her and Sophie in the park on Wednesday evening. But he was glad for any opportunity to distract himself from thinking about how he could only drag things out with his family for so long. Eventually, he'd run out of excuses for not returning home.

Dr. Burgess had also advised him of her plan to retire and sell the business sooner rather than later. He and Bridget avoided discussing what this would mean, but he could tell by her demeanor that she also knew and was concerned. It bothered him more than he wanted it to. He already had so much to deal with, but, each day, his admiration for her kindness to clients, animal and human, grew, along with his gratitude for her kindness to Delilah.

People meant well, but Sawyer was struck with just how rare and refreshing it was to have someone who simply let his daughter *be* without bombarding them with ideas on how they could get her talking again.

He wondered what the wound was that gave Bridget her empathy.

He saw Bridget and Sophie from a distance, heading in their direction. Even from far away, he could sense a lighter mood, as if she felt protected enough by the distance between them to let down her perpetual guard. He couldn't actually see her expression, of course, but there was a bounce in her step and she held her head high, her blond hair floating out behind her, while the gentle breeze played with it.

It was beautiful hair and every time he saw Bridget he fleetingly imagined how it would feel slipping between his fingers.

Sawyer shook his head sharply. *That* was the last place he wanted or needed to go. Yet, as they got closer, his rebellious eyes took in the way the pattern on her shirt matched her eyes and the way the summer skirt she wore floated becomingly around her legs.

Apparently he couldn't trust his emotions, so he was glad of the commotion that ensued when Sophie and Delilah spotted each other. Sophie strained rebelliously at the end of her leash as

Delilah raced toward her. As soon as Delilah reached her, Sophie calmed down.

"Do you see that?" Bridget shook her head wonderingly. "I still can't get over the way these two have taken to each other. I should hire Delilah as her trainer," she said only half-jokingly.

"Can we go there?" Delilah pointed to a shady area of trees a short distance away.

"Yes, but just stay where we can see you," Sawyer said.

They found a seat on a nearby bench. He breathed in the delicate scent of apples from Bridget's shampoo.

Bridget stood up again and called out, "Delilah, I forgot to give you something."

Delilah ran over with Sophie following her.

"This is Sophie's favorite ball." Bridget handed her a green tennis ball that looked like it had seen better days. "She likes to play fetch with it."

Bridget sat down again and Sawyer said, "So, you said you had something to discuss with me?"

"I did," Bridget said. "I think we've both heard by now what Doc B's plans are."

"Yes," Sawyer said. "I feel for her. Those situations are never easy."

"Are you still going to make an offer to buy the property?" Bridget's eyes fixed on his.

Her combination of vulnerability and gritty determination compelled him to be honest with her.

"I'm still giving it serious thought."

"Does it have to be that property?" Bridget persisted. "You said you wanted to set up your own investment business." She unzipped her purse and took out a folded piece of paper. "These are some business properties for sale that a friend of mine who's a Realtor emailed to me." She extended the paper to him and, after a slight hesitation, Sawyer took it from her.

"I guess I can have a look," he said.

"I appreciate that," Bridget said.

He couldn't explain his disappointment over the businesslike exchange.

But Bridget's small smile was satisfied as she turned her attention to Delilah and Sophie.

"Your little girl has been very good for Sophie," she said.

Sawyer nodded. "Sophie has been good for Delilah too." He hesitated briefly before adding, "This is the happiest I've seen her since her mother passed away." There were so many other details he could have added to try to explain that Delilah was really only a fragile, imperfect facsimile of the little girl she had been, but he didn't want to go there.

Bridget didn't say anything. That was something else Sawyer appreciated about her: she didn't rush to try to fill the gap of silence.

"I don't mean to overstep," he said after another moment, "but are you saying that you're able to make an offer on the clinic? Is that why you want to give me the opportunity to look at other properties?"

She was silent for a time, staring into the distance.

"I suppose you could say," she said so softly he had to listen very closely to hear her, "that I'm choosing to believe it will all work out."

Bridget's declaration of faith stayed with Sawyer. He didn't know why, but he sensed that her faith was hard-won these days—the way his was.

Later, he prayed that night after he had tucked Delilah in and she had stayed silent through the prayer that she used to recite happily along with both her parents:

Dear Lord,
Help me to know what I should do. I want to
do what's best to help Delilah and me move
forward. But I don't want to hurt my parents.
And, even though I don't know her well, I
don't want to wreck Bridget's dreams either.
You know our hearts, Lord. If there is an an-
swer to all of this, please help me find it.

The next morning, however, his brother, Marc, called again and Sawyer was no closer to getting his answer.

"Just checking in," Marc said, his tone signaling impatience. "Are you getting things wrapped up there?"

"The software will be here by the end of the week, early next at the latest," Sawyer said.

"Dude, you know that's just an excuse," Marc said bluntly. "When have you ever let computer problems or anything else keep you from doing your job? Dad's out of the office this morning, so let's talk. What's really going on?"

"What's Dad doing?" Sawyer asked, steering the conversation in another direction because he didn't know how much of an answer he wanted to—or could—give Marc.

"He had a doctor's appointment."

Surprise and concern flooded through Sawyer. His father wasn't much for doctors, or anything that impacted getting work done.

"What for?" he asked.

"He said it was just a routine checkup," Marc said.

"So, you haven't noticed anything wrong?"

"Well, we both know he works too hard," Marc said. "He's tired. Mom probably nagged him to go. But, you know, it would give Dad and me a break if you were back here."

Sawyer sighed, as his own tiredness crept through his bones.

"That's what this call is really about, isn't it, Marc? Getting me back to work where I'm supposed to be?"

"Partly that, yeah. I mean why wouldn't we expect that? But also to see what's going on with you. How's the peanut?"

Sawyer reminded himself that, although Marc was a type A personality—highly ambitious and driven, like their father—he did love Delilah and was concerned about her.

"She's actually doing well here," Sawyer said, thankful for an opening that might give him a chance to explain why they needed a change so badly. "She's formed this amazing bond with this golden retriever, a rescue dog that belongs to Bridget..."

"Who's Bridget?" Marc interjected.

"She works at the animal clinic where I'm doing that audit."

"Ahh."

"What does that mean?"

"I think it means I know why you're not in a rush to come home."

"It has nothing to do with that," Sawyer said sharply. "She's just someone I've been working with. You asked how Delilah's doing and I'm trying to tell you."

"Just pushing your buttons, dude." Marc laughed. "And apparently it worked. I'm glad Delilah's having some fun. Poor kid deserves it." He sobered. "But you know you've got to get back here, right?"

"I just want to take it one day at a time for now," Sawyer said. "I think I deserve that too." He rarely played the widower's card, but everything was crowding in on him like a vise clamp on his nerves.

He thanked his brother for the call and hung up, wondering how accurate it was to describe Bridget as just someone he was working with. Of course, that's all she was but when he pictured her smile any clear definitions were obscured by clouds of confusion.

While he ate his breakfast, Sawyer kept his word to Bridget and looked over the list of properties she'd given him.

"Do you know where these are?" he asked Mildred. One of the nice things about Mildred was that she was always willing to answer questions without pushing for why the answers were needed.

She looked the list over. "None on Main Street," she said. "There's a couple on the outskirts of town."

So it remained that the current location of the clinic was a premium piece of real estate.

Would it make any sense at all for him to give that up? But, then again, did it make any sense for him to stay at all?

He found Delilah in her room, sitting cross-legged on the bed and turning the pages of a picture book that featured a romping, spotted dog on the cover.

"Uncle Marc phoned," Sawyer said.

She looked up, her expression one of mild interest.

"He asked how you're doing," Sawyer said. "Everyone misses you."

She nodded and went back to turning the pages of her book.

"Dee-Dee, what do you think about us going home soon?"

Her eyes wide, she shook her head with a ferocity that unhinged him.

In Green Valley there were unanswered questions, complicated decisions. But at home the answer was grief, the shadow of his little girl and a business he could no longer put his heart into.

It appeared God wasn't going to provide any easy answers.

Bridget checked the clock in the clinic. It was almost 9:00 a.m. Sawyer and Delilah should be arriving soon and she planned to suggest that they walk Sophie before the first appointment. It would give her a chance to get Sawyer's thoughts on the properties without Dr. Davidson in hearing distance.

In whatever spare moments she'd had between work and classes, she had been trying her best to formulate a business plan and to brainstorm ideas to raise funds for a down payment. So far, however, the slate remained discouragingly blank. And Dr. Burgess's recent decision to retire effective immediately meant that the clock was ticking.

She'd been both organizer and participant in many fundraisers over the years, but those were generally to do with something that impacted the entire town, not to help an individual make her own dreams come true.

When Sawyer and Delilah arrived, Bridget glanced up and immediately noticed how good Sawyer looked with his hair slightly tousled from the summer morning breeze and the way the light orange, short-sleeved shirt he wore showed off the tan he was getting. But what was more attractive than that was that he treated her with respect; he was willing to at least consider what she wanted, something Wes never did.

The unwelcome thought of Wes reminded her that she had no intentions of fully trusting a man, not ever again. Sawyer might be pleasant and respectful, but he also had his own agenda.

"Hi, Delilah," she greeted the little girl, not allowing her thoughts to slide in a negative direction.

Delilah smiled and gave a little wave.

"I thought we'd take Sophie for a walk first," Bridget said. "Would you like that? I'd like you to come too," she added to Sawyer. "It will give us a chance to talk."

Sawyer nodded. "I did look at the properties like you asked," he said.

Sophie came wagging forward. Her face was proud and solemn, and her cheeks bulged.

"What have you got now?" Bridget asked, lifting the dog's ears and giving the soft spots beneath them a little scratch.

Sophie's doggy grin showed her favorite green tennis ball.

"Delilah, can you please ask Sophie to give you the ball like I taught you?" Bridget said.

"Out," whispered Delilah.

"A little louder," Bridget encouraged, wishing she knew the secret behind Delilah's unwillingness to talk and that she could help in some way. "And hold out your hand."

"Out!" Delilah repeated in a slightly louder tone and Sophie let the ball fall out of her mouth. It rolled across the floor and Delilah chased after it, with Sophie leaping behind, almost upending a rack of brochures.

"Did you notice her hair?" Sawyer asked, stepping forward to prevent the rack from falling.

"Hair?" Bridget repeated, distracted.

"Delilah's ponytail," Sawyer explained. "She asked Mildred to make her one. I think she wanted to look like you."

"I'm flattered about the hairstyle," Bridget said. "But it wasn't that long ago that she was sporting Mildred's braids," she quipped to hide the poignant tugging at her heart.

She clipped on Sophie's leash, using it as an excuse to hide her face. Delilah took the leash eagerly and went to wait at the front door of the clinic.

"How did your wife like Delilah to wear her hair?" she asked, when the little girl was out of hearing distance.

Outside, Delilah and Sophie walked a little way ahead of them. Sawyer didn't answer right away and Bridget worried she'd overstepped a boundary.

"Tina always wanted Delilah to look like a little girl in a storybook," Sawyer finally answered. "She loved her so much but I don't think she got what she imagined in a daughter." His smile was so sad that Bridget blinked back answering tears. "You wouldn't know this now, but Delilah was such a loud little tomboy. She loved running and sports and anything she could get her hands on to muck around or take apart. They didn't always see eye to eye, that's for sure. But Delilah gets her love of books and animals from her mother."

"She sounds like she was a good mother, a good person," Bridget said.

"She was," Sawyer said quietly. "She was always there. I tried to be a good parent too, but I had other obligations on me with the family business and all. I still do." His face drooped with regret.

"Anyone can see how much being a good father to Delilah means to you," Bridget said.

"It's nice of you to say so," Sawyer said. "It's been difficult for us."

Silenced pulsed between them, heavy with all the words he couldn't say.

"I'm an only child like Delilah," Bridget offered.

"Were you spoiled rotten?" Sawyer teased, seeming relieved that the previous subject had been dropped.

"No," Bridget said, not quite able to match his joking tone. "But my parents want me to be happy."

Her stomach clenched. She wished she could give them that.

"So, you said that Delilah gets her love of books and animals from her mother, but she must get her love of music from you?" She changed the subject again, but this time for her own sake.

"I've always liked music," Sawyer said. "It's more of a recent thing for Delilah, although she does have a natural ear for it."

"Did you take any kind of music lessons?" Bridget asked. "Do you play anything?"

"Piano and guitar," Sawyer said. "At one time, I actually thought I might make some kind of a career out of music, like teaching it, or at least volunteering with a worship team at a church or something."

"You still could," Bridget said.

"It's not practical," Sawyer said, reiterating their earlier conversation but still not sounding like he believed that assessment.

Bridget opened her mouth to tell him that he had every right to follow his own path in life, then snapped it shut again. She was hardly the person to be giving that kind of advice.

"Were you about to say something?"

"Just that we were going to talk about the properties," she improvised.

"I did look," Sawyer said again. "I even asked Mildred some questions about them."

"But…" Bridget said.

"But the locations aren't great," Sawyer said.

So they were back to square one.

She shook off the despondency that wanted to envelop her like a dark cloak.

"There's really no such thing as a bad location in Green Valley," she said, trying to sound authoritative. "If you got to know people—if they got to know you and trust you—if they wanted your services, they would find you. You said you wanted to know more about the town, to get to know the people."

"I did say that," Sawyer agreed. "I just don't want…"

Bridget hurried on before she could hear something that would permanently dash her fragile hope.

"There are activities tonight at the church I attend—Green Valley Community Church. They're usually on Wednesdays but things got switched around for a council meeting. It's a great place to get a feel for the community and there are stories and crafts for the kids. As a matter of fact, I'm scheduled to lead them tonight. Tyson will be there, if Delilah's worried about not knowing anyone."

"If I can convince Delilah it's a good idea, maybe we can give it a try," Sawyer said.

Ahead of them, Delilah and Sophie reached the corner and Delilah stopped and waited for them to catch up, smiling at them over her shoulder.

Bridget saw Sawyer's answering smile and again knew he would do what it took to bring happiness back into his daughter's life. Well, she didn't want anything else to hurt Delilah either, which was why she was trying to find an answer that could work for all of them.

Yes, if she kept telling herself that it was about Delilah, she could ignore the long buried but far from unpleasant sensation she got when a gentle hint of Sawyer's spicy aftershave drifted to her on the summer-morning breeze.

Chapter Seven

Delilah planted her foot on Sawyer's knee and bounced it impatiently waiting for him to tie her shoelaces. He was happy that she was willing to go to the church for the activities, but it meant that he couldn't use her as an excuse for his own uneasiness.

But, Lord, how long have I been doing that?

He knew he had to be the adult and make a decision about where they were going to live and what kind of life they would have there. Delilah was only seven years old. She might kick up a fuss, but ultimately it was up to him to decide what was best for her in the long run.

But his attraction to Bridget Connelly wasn't helping matters either.

And now, to add to everything else, he wasn't feeling sure at all about this visit to her church.

Although he continued to pray, he hadn't set

foot in a church since Tina's funeral. He knew that his family and friends at home assumed he was angry with God and there was some truth in that. But there was something else, deeper and more complicated, that couldn't be summed up by labeling his emotions with anger, or even grief. It was more like sheer bewilderment. It didn't matter how often people said that being a Christian didn't mean an easy road in life—he wondered how many of them had secretly believed that it did give them some kind of pass on misfortunes. He'd certainly held that view, until something devastating came along to blindside him and throw his faith off balance.

His shoelace tying duties complete, Sawyer lifted Delilah's foot off his knee and stood up.

"Let's go, Daddy," she whispered. She wore pink shorts and a light blue blouse and her hair still swung in the ponytail that matched Bridget's. Sawyer thought of Tina's brown hair, always professionally highlighted and cut in the latest style, and he stopped himself from making a comparison.

"Do you need to use the bathroom before we go?" Sawyer heard his own voice rising, louder than necessary, as if by doing so he could force his daughter to speak at a normal volume.

The memory of that horrible day swept over him, as immediate as his most recent breath.

Sometime later he had told Marc that it was like the air had been sucked right out of the house.

He walked toward the kitchen, calling their names as a sense of unease such as he'd never experienced before crawled over him like a hideous creature. He saw Tina slumped on the floor, unmoving, and he called her name over and over; he could hear a voice that couldn't possibly be his getting louder and louder. He shook her gently, then roughly, to no avail.

Then finally, in the silence came Delilah's whisper, both childlike and somehow very, very old. "I yelled at Mommy and she fell over."

Sawyer felt an impatient tug on his hand that snapped him back into the present. Delilah was letting him know that she was ready to go.

When they entered the church a little while later, Sawyer's skin prickled with nervousness. Delilah took in their surroundings with an expectant look. Tina and Delilah had always loved church, he recalled with a sweet, sorrowful pang. He had enjoyed attending, but what he really loved was standing beside his beautiful wife in the service as she sang the praise music. She had never let being tone-deaf dampen her enthusiasm. After service they would pick up Delilah from Sunday school and listen to her chatter about the things she had learned.

Sawyer relaxed his tense shoulders, remembering how good those days had been…until he remembered bitterly that not even Delilah had been allowed to keep that unquestioning faith.

He forced himself to focus on their current surroundings, so that his anger and grief didn't overwhelm him.

He liked what he saw. The hall was large, spacious and functional with generous windows that allowed a lot of natural light to flow in. Dress was casual and people were milling about doing a variety of things from chatting in groups to moving tables and chairs and carrying a variety of sports equipment outside.

"Let's go find Bridget," Sawyer said, not wanting to be swarmed by well-meaning people who wanted to greet the strangers in their midst.

Delilah nodded and bounced a little.

Downstairs, where the children's activities took place, he saw Tyson and Paul Belvedere.

Tyson spotted them and ran over to greet them.

"Hi," he said. "The story's gonna be great tonight and Bridget said we could use clay to make stuff after and Max is here, that's my other friend who's a girl, plus Michael might come." The little boy chatted so fast he didn't seem to notice or care that Delilah just listened intently, her head tilted to one side.

Bridget came out of one of the rooms and

her eyes sought his. Sawyer was startled by a jolt of familiarity: the kind of sensation he used to get when he was somewhere with Tina and their eyes would meet and everything would feel right in his world.

For the longest time he had believed that with Tina gone he would never experience that again.

He couldn't let himself believe that he had a real connection with someone he barely knew when he didn't trust his own instincts. He shrugged off the urge to hurry to her and blurt out everything he was thinking and feeling, and instead gave a casual wave.

She raised her eyebrows at him and appeared about to say something, but then turned her attention on the children instead.

"Hi, Delilah. Hi, Tyson. Would you like to come in? The room's all ready now. Tyson, could you please introduce Delilah to the other kids?"

Tyson nodded.

"Wait a second, please," Sawyer said. He clutched Delilah's hand, as if he was the child plagued by separation anxiety.

"Is everything okay?" Bridget asked.

"Can I talk to you?" Sawyer mumbled. "Over here?" He moved a few steps away and Bridget followed.

"What's up?" She folded her arms.

"I'm worried that Delilah won't feel comfortable with the other kids."

"I know she's shy by nature," Bridget said in a reassuring way. "Everyone is shy at first, but the kids here are great and Tyson will help."

Bridget meant well, but Delilah *wasn't* shy by nature. Before her mother's death, she would have taken over the room. But that was too complicated to explain to Bridget, even if he wanted to.

"I guess I'm just being an overprotective parent," he said.

"You're welcome to stay if it makes you feel better," Bridget said. "We can always use an extra hand for crowd control."

"Crowd control?"

She laughed. "Yes, even a few kids at this age can feel like a crowd."

Sawyer remembered Delilah and her friends storming into their kitchen, a chattering mob seeking food and drink.

"I know," he said softly.

"You could come in and see how it goes," Bridget urged. "You can stay as long as you like, or you can find something to do that you're interested in. Some of the guys here like to practice music in the fellowship hall. There's a piano there. You'd be welcome to join them. Our session never goes over an hour, so come back whenever you like."

"Okay," Sawyer agreed. "I'll come in for a few minutes first and make sure she's doing okay."

Tyson took his assignment seriously and introduced Delilah to the other children with a friendly flair. Soon they were all seated in a semicircle ready to hear the story of Noah's ark. Sawyer could see that Delilah was enthralled by the tale and didn't need him there. He caught Bridget's eye and gestured with his head toward the door, letting her know he was ready to slip out.

She nodded and the smile she gave him added an extra layer of reassurance.

Sawyer wandered through the church returning the greetings of the curious but friendly people. He was relieved when he saw the familiar faces of Paul Belvedere and Seth Acoose.

"A first-timer," Seth greeted him when he joined them. "Great to see you."

"Tyson will be happy Delilah is here," Paul added.

"I was a bit nervous about leaving Delilah," Sawyer confessed. He chuckled. "Just call me helicopter dad."

"Oh, I hear you," Paul said. "I was the same way with Tyson. I'm starting to lighten up a bit. But Bridget's on story time tonight, isn't she?

You don't have a thing to worry about. She has a real heart for the kids."

The words were like the gentle pressure of a reassuring hand on Sawyer's shoulder. It wasn't just further evidence that Bridget did have a rapport with Delilah; it was being able to talk about such a thing in the first place. He'd sat through countless business meetings and never once would it have occurred to him to share with anyone that he was a worried father.

"There's a group of us meeting outside to play basketball," Paul said. "You're welcome to join."

"Thanks," Sawyer said. "But I heard I could join in with some music?"

"You bet," Seth said. "I have to talk to the choir director about something, so I'm headed that way."

"Thanks, sounds good."

Paul waved. "Probably see you picking up Delilah."

Seth introduced Sawyer to the group and he was readily welcomed to sit at the piano. The hour passed quickly and Sawyer couldn't remember the last time he let himself enjoy being in the moment. The notes they played were sweetened by his trust that Delilah was in good hands.

"You play a pretty decent piano." The slightly stout white-haired man who had been on the trumpet stepped up and offered his hand. "Harold Price. I own the garage here in town, so if your car is giving you any trouble while you're here, I'm your guy."

Sawyer shook his hand. "Price? So you must be Mildred's brother?"

Harold was notably shorter and wider than Mildred, but their blue eyes snapped with the same straightforward kindness and curiosity.

"My daughter and I are staying with Mildred," Sawyer explained.

Harold nodded. "Yep, I'm aware."

Of course he was.

"I also hear you're working with Bridget Connelly at the animal clinic," Harold added. "How's that going?"

"Can you walk with me?" Sawyer asked, glancing at the clock. "I have to pick Delilah up from the story time."

"Sure," Harold agreed.

As they walked, Sawyer filled Harold in on the computer problems and how it had delayed his work, adding, "But I'm not really in a rush to go home, to be honest. This change of pace has been good for us."

He didn't say anything about wanting to make an offer on the clinic, because he didn't know how public it was yet that Dr. Burgess planned to sell. Besides, he already sensed that Harold wouldn't be too keen on his conflict with Bridget over it.

As if he knew his thoughts, Harold asked. "How are you and Bridget getting along? My sister thinks there might be a spark between the two of you."

"A spark?" Sawyer repeated, aware that his mouth was gaping. He snapped it shut. "We're working together, that's all. I mean we're civil and my little girl absolutely loves that dog of hers and the feeling there seems to be mutual, but I don't think Bridget even likes me all that much, which is fine because, like I said…"

Stop babbling, Sawyer told himself.

"You're just working together," Harold said, his eyes twinkling. "Look," he said, more seriously, "maybe Bridget isn't very friendly these days but that's because she's still hurting over that relationship she got out of, which we all suspect was a nasty one. I mean, she'd never say so, she doesn't talk about it. But, I tell you, that girl's got the warmest heart of anyone you'd ever want to meet."

"I'm sure that's true," Sawyer said. He wanted to tread lightly. He suspected he knew what Harold was driving at but there was no way he was looking for something like that.

Which raised the question: if they did stay

in Green Valley, was this well-intentioned but meddling interest what he could expect?

And the other, deeper question: why was he compelled to protest so strongly about having any feelings toward Bridget?

As Bridget helped the kids clean up after their crafts, she kept an eye on the door and wondered how Sawyer had kept himself busy for the past hour.

She didn't quite understand the small thud her heart made when he came into the room, but she was thankful he only had eyes for his daughter.

"How did it go, Dee-Dee?" Sawyer swept her up in a high arc above his head, eliciting a small squeak, before setting her down again. "Did you have fun?"

Delilah nodded and took him by the hand to show him the clay figures she'd made.

"She did have fun," Bridget agreed. "She loved the story time and she enjoyed working with the clay afterward."

Sawyer lowered his voice. "Um, don't quote me on this but what exactly *are* those things she made?"

"They're giraffes." Bridget smiled.

"Of course—my bad." Sawyer nodded solemnly and Bridget giggled.

When was the last time a man had made her giggle?

"I see you and your little girl both survived," Paul said to Sawyer.

Bridget was relieved to see Paul for reasons she wouldn't name.

"Dad!" Tyson ran over. "We had the best time. Bridget did all the voices when she read the story."

"All the voices?" Sawyer raised his eyebrows at her. "And what voices would those be?"

"The animals," Tyson said.

"I wasn't aware the animals on the ark had all that much to say." Sawyer folded his arms and studied her. The grin on his face caused her stomach to flutter.

Bridget's cheeks flushed. "Sometimes I like to ad-lib a bit," she said. "The kids get a kick out of it."

"Please do one of the voices for me," Sawyer requested.

"Do the elephant," Tyson shouted excitedly and Delilah jumped up and down clapping her hands. A few other parents and children milled about, but paused as the exchange caught their attention.

But it was like a dome had dropped over Sawyer and her and it was just them alone in the room.

Bridget's thoughts and heart raced. It was such a silly request. Wes never would have asked her to behave in a silly manner. Instead, he would have lashed out, lambasting her if he thought she'd embarrassed him.

Now Sawyer was asking her to drop her guard and show him the silly side of her. But there was nothing mean or malicious in the challenge. There was only the sense that he wanted to get to know her on another level.

She took a deep breath. "I hope they don't make us sleep by the monkeys," she boomed in a sonorous voice. "They'll keep us up all night with their chattering."

Sawyer's burst of admiring laughter warmed her. It was like shedding off a ponderous garment for some lighter, more comfortable clothing.

"Don't expect that level of performance when I read next week," Paul chuckled, reminding Bridget that there were others in the room.

"We're very happy to have you read for us, Paul," Bridget said. She smiled at the formerly illiterate man. Paul and her cousin Charlotte had fallen in love when she taught him how to read.

Tyson tugged on his dad's sleeve to get him to bend down and whispered something in his ear.

"Tyson wants to know if Delilah would like to join us for ice cream," Paul said as he straightened up again. "It would be my treat and I could drop her off when we're done. It won't be late."

"Would you like to go?" Sawyer asked his daughter.

She nodded, smiling.

Bridget saw Sawyer tug at his lower lip, but then he rallied.

"Thank you very much," he said. "Next time it's on me."

After everyone had left, Bridget put the remainder of the craft supplies away, all too aware of Sawyer's continued presence in the room.

When she finally turned to look at him he was shuffling his feet. "Looks like I've found myself with some free time," he said.

"I have to lock up," Bridget said, not wanting to read anything into his statement.

"How did you spend your time here?" she asked, as they walked down the hallway and up the stairs to the main hall of the church.

"I found the music group," Sawyer answered. "I played the piano. They want me to join them again. They said they give fundraising concerts sometimes."

"You'd have to plan to stick around for one of those," Bridget mused, her muscles tensing.

He wasn't keen on any of the other properties, which could only mean that he still had an eye on Dr. Burgess's clinic. The heavy cloak settled again.

It wasn't that she disliked Sawyer. No, she liked him more than she wanted or expected to. But that didn't change the fact that he was a big obstacle in the way of her goals.

Dear Lord, I have to find a way to make an offer on the clinic. Please guide my thoughts. Help me to think clearly, to come up with ideas.

The one option she wasn't willing to consider was asking her parents for money, even though she knew they would be happy to help her. But she needed to do this on her own as part of her growing process.

"This was fun," Sawyer said outside the church. "Thank you for suggesting it."

She nodded. "You're welcome."

"Are you in a rush to get home?" Sawyer asked. He glanced at her and then at his feet.

He was at loose ends, Bridget thought, lifting up her hand to touch his arm and then rapidly dropping it. He might be a businessman who was potentially after the same property she was, but in that moment he was simply a man who had not expected his little girl to have an outing without him.

Bridget had been looking forward to getting home to enjoy a glass of lemonade and the last few chapters of the cozy mystery she was reading, but Sawyer's plight evoked sympathy.

"We could take Sophie for a walk," she suggested. "I'll just send Paul a quick text to let him know, though I'm sure you'll beat Delilah home." She pulled out her phone and began messaging.

"That sounds like a plan." Sawyer's face brightened.

"You can just wait here," Bridget said, when they reached her house. Her mother's coaching on company manners always gave her a little stab of guilt when she didn't invite someone in, but the last time a man was in her house he had slapped her, stripping away the gift of security that she believed she'd had in her own home. The worst had passed but having a man on her doorstep momentarily brought the darkness rushing back.

"We don't have to do this," Sawyer said hesitantly, and she realized that she had gone rigid, her hand frozen on the door handle.

Bridget gave her head a quick shake. "Daydreaming. I'll be right back." Daydreaming was an odd way to describe a nightmarish memory.

Thankfully, Sophie's joy at seeing her worked its power and chased away the temporary darkness.

"Hey, girl." She knelt down and let the dog

hurtle into her arms. "Yes, I'm home and guess what? We're going for a walk. Go get your leash."

If it was possible for the dog to get any more excited than she already was, those words sent Sophie leaping like a giant, clumsy rabbit in the direction of her leash. She returned with it in her mouth.

"Good girl," Bridget praised.

"Hey, Soph." Sawyer greeted her when they came outside. He reached out and she allowed him to scratch her head, even rewarding him with a doggy grin.

"See?" He smiled at Bridget. "I knew I'd win her over."

The words hung between them as their gazes met.

"Let's go," Bridget said abruptly, setting the pace and leaving Sawyer behind, but only momentarily, before his long-legged strides caught up with her.

The paths in the park were fairly quiet, except for a small group of walkers some distance ahead of them and the occasional cyclist biking by.

They strolled a few steps in silence while Sophie strained at her leash and panted exuberantly.

"Do you want me to take her?" Sawyer offered. "It looks like she's pulling hard."

"It's okay," Bridget said. "Thanks, but I'm used to it and she's used to me."

"So, you don't think her love for Delilah spills over to me?" Sawyer asked.

She knew he was teasing but nonetheless felt a quiver in her stomach.

"It's probably more that Delilah and I don't remind her of anyone who hurt her." She decided to give his teasing question a serious answer and stay far away from talk that even hinted at anything personal between them. "I think the person who abandoned her was an adult male, or that she was mistreated by one prior to that, maybe both."

"You're probably right," Sawyer said.

They were silent again and, stealing a glance at him out of the corner of her eye, Bridget had the feeling that he was about to say something.

Sophie suddenly lunged at a squirrel and she tightened her grip, using both hands on the leash.

"Whoa, there," Sawyer said, reaching out to help, but she instinctively swayed back from him.

"It's okay," she said hurriedly. "I've got it."

"You know a lot of people in town think very highly of you," he said after a moment.

Bridget's laugh was nervous, stalling a bit in her throat. "Well, we all care for each other, like I've said."

It just made her too uneasy to think of Sawyer discussing her with people she'd known her whole life. It made him too much a part of things, like someone who could stay and put her life in an upheaval.

The worst of it was that she was no longer sure if the upheaval was only about potentially losing out on the clinic.

"Why haven't you made an offer on the clinic?" she blurted out, tilting her head to one side. A thread of tension ran through her neck and shoulders.

"I haven't decided what I'm going to do," Sawyer said with a thoughtful expression. "There's a lot to consider. A change would be great and I like what I know about Green Valley so far. But I'm still thinking about what would be best for Delilah over the long term. It's also not that easy to leave family at home behind either." He nervously ran a hand through his hair.

Bridget didn't want to understand his plight. It just made her own emotions more complicated. Yet, she *did* understand. No one lived in a void and, unless one chose to be a completely self-serving person, it wasn't possible to make decisions without thinking of how they would impact others.

She had no intentions of giving up on her goals, but she had no desire to cause problems for Sawyer or Delilah either.

As if sensing the somber mood of her walkers, Sophie was subdued on the way back, sniffing the grass at the edge of the path but not stopping.

At her own house, a slowly building headache interfered with Bridget's reading enjoyment, until she finally gave up and decided to go early to bed instead. It was probably just as well, with homework and another day of work facing her.

But sleep was a long time coming and any easy answers did not seem to be coming at all.

Chapter Eight

New software was installed on the computer Sawyer was using and it was up and running more efficiently than ever.

He knew he should be happy about this, or, at least relieved, but he could no longer relate to being someone who just wanted to get the job done as efficiently as possible.

Instead, he was caught between a daughter who didn't want to go home and pressure from the rest of his family that he get home sooner rather than later. And, he still couldn't decide if buying the clinic property was worth the upheaval it would cause in Bridget's life.

But maybe the real question was why he cared about that when he really hardly knew Bridget Connelly. He couldn't exactly answer that. It was true that her determination combined with her vulnerability got to him. He was forever changed by Tina's death. It was no longer a cliché to say that life was short, but instead was brutally true, and he could no longer make decisions for business reasons alone.

One good thing was that Delilah was in a happy mood that morning. Tyson and Max, a little girl with delicate features and an unexpectedly deep voice, were coming over to play, and Mildred had promised them that they could explore the attic and then have a picnic in the backyard for lunch.

She'd be so much happier if she could stay here and go to the same school as Tyson and the other kids she's meeting here.

But was that really true? Delilah seemed happier than she had been in Saskatoon but still wasn't using her full voice. Unhappiness, he knew, wasn't something you could run away from and maybe he was just postponing the inevitable.

"Sawyer, I need a favor," Bridget said, interrupting his thoughts. "I was hoping to give Sophie a quick bath before we open. I've tried doing it at home and I can't manage her in my bathtub. I really just need someone to help me get her in and out of a tub. Dr. Davidson is going to be late getting in and I thought it would be a good time to get it done."

She said it all in a rush, clearly not at ease with asking him for help.

"And why, exactly, is it so important that she have a bath today?" Sawyer asked, to take the pressure out of the moment. "Does she have a date tonight?"

Bridget laughed and the sound was like a balm to his spirit.

"It's good to hear you laugh," Sawyer said. He clamped his mouth shut. The observation seemed too intimate, especially with Bridget's steady, questioning gaze on his face.

"It's good *to* laugh," she finally answered. "But, in answer to your question, I advise staying downwind of her. She found something… ah—unique—to roll in last night."

"Ah, gotcha," Sawyer said. "Okay, Sophie, let's get you beautiful."

As if knowing she was being talked about, Sophie rolled her eyes upward and sideways, then, like a magician, opened her mouth and a pen fell out.

"Where in the world did you get that?" Bridget shook her head. "Come on, Soph." She wrapped her fingers around the dog's collar and gave a gentle pull.

Sawyer followed them to a back room where they both donned waterproof aprons.

After some struggle—Bridget was right, it was a two-person job—they maneuvered Sophie into a tub and she now wore a crown of frothy suds and a look of embarrassment.

"I can handle it from here," Bridget said. But as soon as Sawyer removed his hands from the trembling dog, Sophie tried to scramble out of the tub again.

"I'll stay," Sawyer said.

The strange familiarity of sharing a task with someone both comforted and saddened Sawyer.

Dear God, could I ever share my heart again?

Even asking the question surprised him.

He noticed some bubbles on Bridget's nose and grinned.

"What's so funny?" she asked suspiciously.

"You've got a big dab of soap on your nose," he said.

"I do?" She started to reach her hand up to her nose, but his hand got there first.

"Yes," he said. "Right here." He touched her nose lightly with the tip of his finger.

Bridget pulled back so suddenly that she fell, losing her hold on Sophie, and chaos ensued. Sophie, startled by the sudden motion, sprung out of the tub and circled the room, her feet skidding out in all different directions on the wet floor. She shook herself vigorously, sending sprays of water and soap flying everywhere.

I didn't mean to scare her. Sawyer's thoughts spun like the agitated dog.

At last, Sophie found her way back to him in a cringing kind of crawl, letting him comfort her like he'd always been her most trusted friend.

"It's okay," he said in a soft, soothing voice. "It's okay, don't be afraid. You don't have to be afraid anymore."

For a fleeting moment, Bridget looked at him like she wondered if he was talking to her.

Sophie flopped down and began to nibble at her paws and Sawyer went back to the tub and began to mop the water up with a towel.

"We'll have to get her rinsed off somehow," he commented, with his back to Bridget.

"Yes," Bridget answered. Her voice was devoid of emotion. "There's no point cleaning up the water now," she added. "Like you said, we have to rinse her off."

With a minimal exchange of words, they managed to coax Sophie back into the tub, finished off her bath and cleaned up the area together, placing their aprons on a nearby rack when they were done.

All the while, the words that weren't being said hung between them like weights strung on the most fragile of threads.

"I shouldn't have assumed that I could touch you," Sawyer said, to end the silence between them. "I just thought you… Never mind." He shook his head. "It was wrong of me to make any kind of assumption without asking and I'm sorry for that."

"I accept your apology," Bridget said. "I probably overreacted."

He waited to see if she would add anything, but all she said was, "I guess we're done here. I mean with the bath."

"I guess we are." So he would be left to wonder why his touch had provoked an almost violent reaction. His thoughts turned again to Harold's remark about a nasty relationship.

Oh, Lord, did someone hurt her?

The idea of it pained him.

He offered to make her tea before going back into his office to get to the work he was in no rush get done.

"No, thank you," Bridget said with a pensive, almost quizzical expression. "It's nice of you to offer, though."

In the office, Sawyer started up the computer and the spreadsheet he needed rapidly loaded.

But instead of entering numbers, he sat and thought again about what had just happened. And about how he would never want to do anything that would hurt Bridget in any way.

God, I can't keep reacting from a place of distrust. I've asked You to heal me. What is it going to take? Because even though the logical part of her knew that Sawyer wasn't Wes, Bridget's mind strayed back to Wes's constant criticisms and the moment of that dreadful slap: sometimes she could still hear the sound his palm made striking the side of her cheek, still feel the cold shock that ripped through her.

You need to tell your family the truth about your relationship.

Every time she prayed, she got the same answer and it was in line with the advice she was getting at support group. But she just couldn't bring herself to do it. Her family had climbed over some dreadful hurdles to reach a point of contentment in their lives and she didn't want to be the person to ruin that, even if that meant putting up a roadblock to her own healing.

No, it was much better to concentrate on work and her classes, and on figuring out how she could make a down payment on the clinic before it was too late. If Sawyer didn't make a move, someone else was bound to as soon as the property went on the market.

Sawyer...

She didn't even want to think of what a spectacle she must have made of herself. Despite that, she couldn't stop thinking of his scent when they were in close proximity. Laundry detergent and a masculine soap with a slight undertone of spiciness: a scent that made her feel safe…like she could trust him.

Unfortunately, her past relationship guaranteed that trust was still hard to come by, and maybe always would be.

On Saturday, Bridget was meeting Charlotte, her mother and Charlotte's mother for lunch. They'd decided to avoid the Saturday rush at Seth's and instead have the lunch special at the Harvest. The Harvest was an old-style steak house, its atmosphere always dim, even in the daytime, and its serious serving staff in stark contrast with gregarious Seth. But their lunch specials were delicious and the quiet atmosphere was good for visiting.

When she arrived at the restaurant and saw the three of them already at a table, Bridget felt a rush of love and fondness for her family and regretted the time that Wes had kept her mostly separated from them.

She couldn't imagine Sawyer doing that.

But why should she care what he would do?

"Bridget!" Charlotte called and waved. "We're over here. You looked like you were a million miles away."

Bridget smiled and walked quickly to the table.

Her mother stood and kissed her cheek. "Hello, dear."

Bridget hugged her and then leaned down to give her aunt and Charlotte hugs.

"We're just deciding what to order," her mother said. "We thought we'd all have the soup of the day—it's minestrone—and then share a couple of different sandwiches between the four of us. How does that sound? They have chicken salad, which is always good, or roast beef?"

"Both sound good," Bridget said.

A server, who looked like they'd interrupted him from solving world problems, came to take their order.

Their food arrived and teacups were refilled, and they all exclaimed over the savory soup and the delicious fillings in the sandwiches. In between bites, they chatted about various light topics. It was a reprieve Bridget realized she had desperately needed.

Although they all claimed to be too full for dessert, they couldn't resist the chocolate lava cake and agreed to order one to share between them.

Bridget was enjoying a sweet bite when Aunt Lenore turned to her and said, "I was dropping off some books and magazines at Haven Seniors Home and I saw Dr. Burgess there."

Bridget nodded. "She's been off work. Her mother is having a tough time."

"Did you know she plans to sell the clinic?"

Brenda Connelly turned concerned eyes on her daughter. "You never said anything about that. Are you going to be out of a job?"

"Doc B said she'd make sure I was taken care of," Bridget said, knowing she wasn't answering the actual question.

This was Green Valley, so it wasn't realistic to hope that the word wouldn't get out. But she didn't want her mother to worry about her. Her mother and father had such simple wishes in life: to worship God, to keep their family close and to provide a happy, fulfilling life for their only child.

She wanted so badly to live a life that honored their dream for her.

"She said she's even considering a buyer from Alberta," Aunt Lenore continued. "Someone who has a successful chain of sporting goods stores there and wants to expand into Saskatchewan."

The cake was suddenly dry and tasteless on Bridget's tongue. She had an overwhelming urge to question Sawyer. Why hadn't he made a move on buying the clinic? Had he just tossed the idea out there to taunt her? Yet the more she knew of him, the less she believed that was his style.

But now maybe they were both going to lose the property to someone who would come in and disrupt the flow of Main Street, someone who would likely maintain their home base and never really become part of the community.

Her mind raced, trying to determine the best course of action.

"Are you okay, Bridge?"

Bridget looked up from the fork she still held aloft, into Charlotte's concerned gaze.

"I was just surprised to hear Doc B is thinking of selling to someone outside the community."

"I can't imagine who here would buy it, though," Aunt Lenore remarked. "Everyone is settled in what they're doing."

I can't imagine either, Bridget thought, momentarily allowing herself to succumb to self-pity.

But she shook it away just as quickly. She wasn't going to give in.

"But you did say everything is going to be all right with your job?" Bridget's mother asked.

Brenda Connelly was slightly plump, soft looking, with round, always slightly anxious-looking eyes, and Bridget always wanted to protect her mother from unnecessary stress.

So she said, with more certainty than she currently felt, "Of course, I'll be okay. Everything's going to work out just fine."

Maybe saying it out loud would make it true.

Bridget finished her tea and made appropriate contributions to the conversation, but her thoughts were elsewhere, planning her next conversation with Sawyer.

Occasionally, she would feel Charlotte's gaze on her and she would smile brightly in her direction, even knowing that it wasn't easy to fool Charlotte.

Sure enough, as they were saying their goodbyes at the door, Charlotte hugged her and whispered, "What's going on with you?"

Bridget stepped back and shook her head. Her face was like a clay mask about to crack from smiling so much. "Just a busy day ahead," she said. "Lots on my mind."

The latter, at least, was true.

Charlotte studied her a moment longer. "You know I'm here if you need me, Bridge. I miss hanging out. We'll have to do that, just us, soon."

Bridget missed the times that she and Charlotte had shared everything.

"I know, Char," she said. "We'll talk soon, I promise."

But right now she was on a mission to find out exactly what Sawyer Blume's plans were.

Chapter Nine

How exactly did the end of July sneak up on them? Sawyer wondered.

They were finishing up lunch: toasted tomato sandwiches made with delectable tomatoes from Mildred's garden and, for dessert, fresh blueberries on vanilla ice cream.

"Can you pass the blueberries please, Dee-Dee?" Sawyer asked. Delilah nodded and promptly passed the bowl his way.

The best reason to stay in Green Valley was there in his daughter. She was still not completely herself, she still wasn't using her voice much, but she was tanned and her hair was neatly braided and her smile was ringed with the purple-blue shade of the fruit she'd just passed to him.

It was a brief reprieve to fortify him before he kept his promise to his mother and phoned his father.

To give Sawyer privacy, Mildred engaged Delilah at the kitchen sink, helping her up onto a stool beside her and making the dishwater extra sudsy for her to splash her hands in.

Sawyer retreated to the front room and apprehensively called the business. He wanted to make sure he got directly through to his dad because if his mother answered the phone, he might lose his incentive.

To his surprise, the business phone went to voice mail.

Taking a deep breath, he called the house phone. His father picked up on the first ring.

"Why aren't you home yet?" Hank Blume asked, skipping formalities.

"There have been some complications," Sawyer said, an easy way to sum up everything from the computer crash to the fact that he might be staying…to *There's this woman who's kind of gotten under my skin.*

Was that true?

"Complications are just hurdles to jump over," Hank barked. Sometimes, if Marc was taking a break from idolizing their father, he and Sawyer would joke that their dad often talked like he was a motivational business poster. But his amusement fled quickly when Hank's next sentence was cut off as the wince of physical pain came into his voice.

"Are you okay, Dad?"

"Of course I'm okay!" Sawyer could practically see his father making a dismissive hand gesture.

But Sawyer didn't believe him. Hank Blume was someone who believed that giving in to illness was a sign of weakness, so he would be the last person to admit if there was anything wrong.

Then again, neither his mother nor Marc had said anything.

Sawyer raked a hand through his hair, wishing that the answer on whether to stay or go home would become clear. He continued to try to pray about it, but it still seemed that God was letting him muddle his way through this one on his own.

He decided to try the blunt approach. "Dad, if you need me to come home because you're having some health issues, please just say so."

"I need you to come home because it's your job," Hank boomed, any sign that he wasn't quite himself entirely gone. "I know you've been through the wringer with losing Tina and all, son, and I'm not saying that wouldn't be a trial for any man. But I've always found it's best to face the responsibilities you have and take care of them. Life has to get back to normal sometime."

But *normal* was a word that Sawyer would never use carelessly again.

"It shouldn't take me much longer to wrap up here," he said. It was true, but he couldn't add the promise that he'd be home soon.

Just as they were closing the conversation, he could distinctly hear the sound of strain in his father's voice, as if he was bracing himself against something painful. Knowing he'd get nothing by continuing to question his father, Sawyer promised himself he would call his mother or Marc later for the real story.

Pinching his bottom lip, he ended the call.

"How did that go?" Mildred asked when he returned to the kitchen.

Sawyer silently told Mildred with a head tilt toward Delilah that he didn't want to talk about it.

He was helping Delilah down from the stool when the doorbell rang.

"I wonder who that could be," Mildred mused, wiping her hands on a towel and going to answer it.

A minute later she returned with Bridget. "Isn't this a nice surprise?" she said, beaming.

Bridget smiled, but her eyes told Sawyer that she wasn't there just to pass the time.

Whatever the reason, Delilah's shy smile said she was happy to see her.

"Sophie is tied to the porch outside," Bridget said. "I'm sorry to just pop in like this, but I was wondering if you and Delilah would like to come for a walk."

Delilah jumped up and down, clapping her hands. Sawyer's heart jumped for a completely different reason, wondering what was on her mind.

Not that he wanted to notice, but she did look particularly pretty in a purple sundress with a matching elastic adorning her lively ponytail.

"It's business," she added as explanation to Mildred. "Otherwise, you'd be welcome to join us. Delilah and Sophie get so wrapped up in each other, they won't pay any attention."

"Oh, you just go ahead," Mildred said. "Don't worry about me. I know you have plenty to talk about."

Sawyer thought she looked a smidgen too pleased at the prospect.

Bridget took a moment to help Delilah secure Sophie's leash around her hand and wrist. "How does the park sound?" Bridget asked, and the little girl nodded happily.

Delilah and Sophie launched off a few paces ahead of them and Sawyer called after her, "Wait for us before crossing any streets."

Delilah threw a jaunty thumbs-up over her shoulder.

"Why haven't you bought the clinic?" Bridget asked. "Unless you've made an offer and Doc B just hasn't said anything to me about it, but I can't imagine that."

So, she wasn't going to waste any time getting to the point.

"I haven't made an offer," Sawyer said.

"So why did you tell me you were going to?" Bridget demanded. "Was it just to cause me unneeded stress?"

"Why would I want to do that?" Sawyer asked, honestly baffled.

She studied him for a moment, then her tense shoulders dropped.

"I'm sorry," Bridget said. "I'm a little wound up. I honestly don't know what I'm going to do." She explained to him what her aunt Lenore had said about running into Dr. Burgess at the nursing home and what she had said about selling the property to the first reasonable offer.

"A sporting goods chain?" she moaned. "At least if you bought the property, you might do something to help maintain the character of Main Street."

"So, I'm not just the big, bad investor?" Sawyer couldn't resist quipping.

But Bridget's grimace quickly sobered him.

"Why haven't *you* made an offer?" he asked gently. "And don't tell me it's because you got a loan turned down at the bank. I don't know you all that well but I can't imagine you giving up that easily."

Her expression hovered between gratitude and suspicion. It saddened him that she accepted a compliment like she'd been handed a foreign object.

"I asked you first," she said, after a couple of seconds. Her bantering tone didn't match the shadows in her eyes.

Sawyer shrugged. "The most honest answer I can give you right now is that I don't know. But, no, I didn't say that just to torment you."

"I didn't really think so," Bridget conceded. "I'm just so frustrated." She balled her hands into fists.

At the corner, Delilah and Sophie skidded to a stop and Delilah turned and waved.

"Why don't you know?" Bridget asked as she and Sawyer caught up with them.

"That's a long story," Sawyer said.

But was it one he wanted to tell? Did he want to open up his personal life to Bridget when she was already taking up too much space in his head?

Thankfully, she didn't press him on it, for the moment at least.

"Can I walk Sophie over there?" Delilah pointed to a grassy area with some trees not far from some benches along the edge of a walking path."

"Yes, but stay where we can see you," Sawyer said.

"Would you like to sit?" He gestured at one of the benches and, after hesitating for a moment, Bridget took him up on it. He sat down too, making sure to maintain distance between them.

They watched Delilah and Sophie play.

"I've been trying to think of ways to come up with the money," Bridget said, still looking off in the direction of the frolicking duo, "and trying to come up with a plan that can convince the bank that I'm worth taking a risk on. But there's uncertainty at work and I have classes on top of that and some heavy exams coming up…"

She shook her head and clamped her mouth shut, clearly troubled that she'd said as much as she had.

"I know a thing or two about business plans," Sawyer said. "I could help with that."

When her blue-eyed gaze shifted to look speculatively at him, he too had the sensation of having said too much.

"Why would you?" The question wasn't exactly an accusation but again it made Sawyer wonder exactly what—or who—had damaged her trust in herself and others.

It was a fair question and he was trying to come up with a good answer for her—and for himself—when Bridget suddenly went rigid and her hands gripped the underside of the bench.

Sawyer saw a tall, dark-haired man coming down the path, some distance away.

"Bridget, what's wrong?"

But she had bolted, slipping into a cluster of trees a few feet behind the bench.

Sawyer's insides churned with indecision. He couldn't leave Delilah unattended, but he couldn't leave Bridget in the state she was in.

"Delilah," he called and waved her over.

Please God, he prayed, unsure of what he was praying for.

Delilah's half jog showed her reluctance, and Sophie ambled behind.

The dark-haired man wished them a good morning as he passed them and continued on his way.

Bridget came out from behind the tree taking deep, slow breaths, her eyes telling a story she couldn't yet find the words for.

His heart went out to her and he wanted nothing more than to take her in his arms, to shelter and protect her from any hurts she'd had in the past and whatever hurts she might have in the future.

But he knew that wasn't possible.

* * *

Bridget continued to take deep breaths, willing herself to calm down and come up with some sort of explanation for her hasty retreat, especially now that she realized that the darkhaired man had only resembled Wes from a distance.

What must Sawyer be thinking of her?

But his eyes were kind.

"What just happened there?" he asked. She hadn't known—or had forgotten—that a man could speak so gently.

Tell him the truth. The thought came so suddenly and sharply that Bridget felt the hair lift on the back of her neck like someone had sneaked up behind her to whisper a secret. But, no, that couldn't possibly be God's answer. Even though the women in her support group said the same thing, it was never what she wanted to hear.

But when she saw the genuine concern that continued to shine from Sawyer's eyes, she considered the relief she might feel at sharing her burden. She could get it all out to someone who didn't know her well enough to be badly impacted by it and still protect her family from the terrible truth.

Delilah and Sophie, as if sensing something, waited quietly, the dog docile as Delilah held her leash.

"I do have something to tell you," she said before she could change her mind. She sought his eyes with hers, wanting to be absolutely sure.

Sawyer waited. It seemed to Bridget like their breathing was synchronized and it was an oddly calming sensation.

"I haven't told my family," Bridget said. "I—I belong to a support group and I've told them but no one else."

"You can trust me," Sawyer said. "I won't say anything."

They returned to the bench and Sawyer gave Delilah permission to go and play with Sophie where they'd been before.

"If you'd known me a year ago," Bridget began, "you would have known a completely different person. I cared about my job but I cared more about dating."

Sawyer's attentive silence encouraged her to continue.

"I wanted what my cousin Charlotte has with Paul. I was dating all the time, trying to meet someone who was right for me. I met some nice guys who treated me well and were interested but I trusted I'd know it when it was completely right for me. Do you believe we know the person we're meant to be with, like Charlotte and Paul do?"

Sawyer cleared his throat. "I know many people believe that."

She studied his face for a moment, trying to decipher his answer, then continued. "Well, as you can imagine, in a town this size, it didn't take long for me to figure out that my soul mate wasn't here. So I cast the net a little wider, as they say."

"Did you get into online dating?" Sawyer asked.

Bridget shook her head. "No, that was never my style. I mean I asked my friends and their boyfriends or husbands if they knew any guys they thought I might hit it off with. So, a few months ago, a friend of mine said that her boyfriend's cousin from Toronto was going to be working for a year in Regina, which isn't far from here, and she thought we might hit it off. Her boyfriend is a decent guy so I figured his cousin would be too."

She watched a ladybug make its determined way up along one of the planks of the bench.

"I was wrong."

Sawyer waited, silently giving support.

Listening to her own voice saying the words was like listening to an old record scratching out a song she wished she could forget.

"At first I did think it was perfect," she said. "I thought that *he*—Wes—was perfect. He was handsome, he was witty and charming, he had a good job—he always had money to spend. He treated me like a princess.

"But, after a few months, things started to change." She noticed her hands balled into fists and told herself to relax them. "It was small things, at first," she continued. "Like he'd make little comments about my clothes, or how I was wearing my hair. I'd tell myself that I was being overly sensitive. That's what *he* would tell me if I was hurt by something he said—that I was overreacting. Pretty soon, it got to be this malicious cat-and-mouse game. He got increasingly insulting, but at the same time made me feel as if I was misinterpreting things. I didn't know whether I was coming or going half the time. I stopped trusting myself."

Bridget's breath went ragged as her body physically recalled the anguish and frustration she'd felt.

Sawyer took both her hands in his and she found she didn't mind. His warm, strong grip was comforting.

"You can stop if you want," he said.

"No," she said as she breathed slowly in and out. "I want to get this out.

"There were so many things," she continued when she was able to. "He would flirt and compliment other women, but tell me I was paranoid if I complained about it. He didn't want me to see my family or friends. Everything was about what he wanted and the worst of it was that he convinced me that I was lucky to have him and that I should be grateful that he put up with me."

"I think that's what happens in an abusive relationship," Sawyer said, his voice very soft. "You lose all perspective."

Bridget nodded. "But the strange thing is, I never thought of myself as being abused because he hadn't hit me, at least not yet. I didn't know there was such a thing as emotional and psychological abuse or how deep and lasting the scars could be."

She raised her head and looked directly into Sawyer's eyes.

"When he did slap me, it was because he wanted me to go put on a different sweater and I didn't want to because we were already running late to the movie we were going to. In some ways—" she stopped and swallowed "—in some ways, I'm glad it happened. It was horrible but it finally opened my eyes to what was really going on. I don't know if I would have been able to face the fact that I was being abused or have done anything about it.

"So…that's my story." An unexpected balm of calmness settled over her. She still couldn't quite believe that she had finally shared it with someone outside her support group.

Thank you for helping me to find the words, Lord, and thank you for Your constant presence.

Sawyer didn't say anything but he extended his hand, open and inviting. She hesitated a moment, then reached out too and allowed his hand to enfold hers.

"I'm so sorry that happened to you," he said.

He still held her hand and Bridget wondered, *What now?* What was the next step after telling someone she hadn't even laid eyes on a few short weeks ago a secret that she wouldn't share with her own family?

Chapter Ten

They sat holding hands in a surprisingly compatible silence.

Sawyer's head was spinning, but he gathered his wits enough to reassure himself that Delilah was still having fun with Sophie. He was grateful for that because he didn't want to leave Bridget, who had the tremulous energy of someone coming out the other side of a nasty flu bug.

"Can I say something?" he asked, after another minute of silence.

She darted a glance his way but said, "Okay."

"I want you to know how much I admire you. How smart and motivated I think you are. To be working and taking classes, to have set goals for yourself."

"Goals that might be slipping away from me," Bridget said.

"Don't," Sawyer said. "Don't do that. You've come such a long way. We can figure this out."

He hadn't thought of himself as a "we," at least not with a woman, since Tina's death.

But was it just a way to postpone making his own decisions?

Bridget let go of his hand and he wasn't prepared for the cold shock of disconnection.

"You confuse me, Sawyer," she said bluntly. "You offer to help me and you encourage me not to give up on my goals. Yet, it's still possible that you could sweep everything I want out from under me."

Sawyer felt strangely disappointed. After what she had shared with him, he didn't think her barriers would go up again so quickly. But did he have the right to expect anything different from her?

Delilah looked over at them and jumped up and down waving her arms high above her head in a back-and-forth motion. Sophie jumped in tandem beside her.

It made him smile but it also made him realize more than ever that Bridget had a point. What exactly was he doing? He couldn't just keep strolling through the days, postponing a decision, because whatever decision he made it was going to impact others.

Before the day was over, he would phone his mom or Marc and find out exactly what was going on with his dad. It might be a relief to have his hand forced. He would just have to accept that whatever happened, it was for the best.

Delilah turned a crooked cartwheel while her best doggy friend yipped encouragingly. He sighed as regret washed through him. *Best for who?*

He turned back to Bridget and couldn't resist asking, "Bridget, are you sure you don't need…more?"

"More of what?" she asked.

His shoulders creeping up to his ears indicated the helplessness he felt. "I don't know—more time to talk?"

"I said everything I want to say," Bridget said, a hint of warning in her smile. "But thanks again for listening. I'm fine now."

Sawyer knew that couldn't be true, but it was clear that Bridget didn't want to say anything more now, or perhaps ever. There was nothing he could do about that, except pray for her and do his best to trust that God was listening.

A small consolation occurred to him: if Bridget knew he was going home and wasn't going to be a threat to her future, maybe she would let him help her. There wasn't anything he didn't think this beautiful, strong survivor could do.

He would just need to convince her of that.

"We should get on with our days," Bridget remarked.

"Dee-Dee," Sawyer called over to his daughter. "Three more throws and then we have to go."

Delilah's face crumpled into disappointment but she nodded reluctantly. He was amused to notice that she was throwing the ball as far as she could each time. But his amusement quickly faded when he thought about how she would react if he had to tell her that it was time to leave Green Valley for good.

They were walking out of the park when Bridget's phone rang. She looked at the screen and her brow furrowed.

"It's Doc B," she said. "She rarely calls on a Saturday unless it's urgent."

She answered her phone and engaged in a short conversation with the doctor. Sawyer tried to gauge the subject of the conversation, but Bridget had retreated into her protective shell again—a place where he now knew how deep the wounds were that she kept hidden.

He heard his own name mentioned and something about early Monday morning.

She hung up and was silent for so long that Sawyer finally had to ask, "What was that all about?"

Bridget turned her face to his, her expression carefully neutral. "She wants us to meet her at the clinic at seven-thirty on Monday morning. She says she's made a decision about the clinic."

Then suddenly the neutrality fell away, replaced by an expression of fear mingled with determination. "I won't let some big store chain come in and take over Main Street. We've got to do something!"

We...

Sawyer definitely wasn't going to be the one to remind her that she considered him her rival.

He only wished he could help her—that she would let him—before it was time to make his reluctant journey home, if it came to that.

He prayed that there was an answer, one that would work for all of them.

When Sawyer and Delilah arrived back at Mildred's, Mildred read the troubled lines of his face with a practiced eye and invited Delilah outside to assist her in taking down sheets and pillowcases that had been gently swaying on the clothesline in the summer breeze.

When Sawyer took out his phone to call Marc, he saw that his brother had tried to call him about half an hour earlier and remembered he had put his phone on silent: another avoidance tactic.

Not bothering to listen to the message, he quickly called back.

Marc answered halfway through the first ring and skipped the formalities. "You got my message?"

"I haven't listened to it," Sawyer said. "I saw you called and I was going to call you anyway."

Marc didn't say anything.

"Marc?" Sawyer asked. "You still there?"

"Yeah, I'm just trying to think of how to say this. Would have been easier if you'd just listened to the message so I don't have to do this twice."

"Do what?" Sawyer's free hand reached up and kneaded the bridge of his nose. "Did something happen to Dad…or Mom?"

"Not exactly, but…you've been taken off the project."

"The project? You mean…?"

"Yeah, the one with our biggest clients. Dad said that if you can't make it a priority, you're obviously not committed enough or focused enough to give it your all and he can't risk you being part of it."

"And he got you to call me to tell me this?" Sawyer said as a certain bitter humor coiled through his stomach.

"You know Dad," Marc said.

Yes, Sawyer knew his father and knew what it meant to be written off by him. In another family, it might be feasible to decide they couldn't work together but their family bonds would still be tight. With Hank Blume, however, those lines would always be blurred. It was entirely possible, Sawyer realized, that his father could be writing him not just out of a business deal, but out of his life.

"Yes, I know Dad," he said. "Don't worry, Marc, I won't shoot the messenger."

They attempted to play catch-up a bit but it was obvious that neither of them were in the mood for small talk.

"I am sorry," Marc said.

"Not your fault, maybe it's for the best," Sawyer said, with a tiny whisper of relief at having the decision taken out of his hands. He asked after their father's health but Marc wasn't able, or wasn't willing, to shed much light.

But maybe the strangest thing was the way his thoughts went immediately to Bridget, after he'd hung up the phone with this brother The strength and grace she showed in leaving an abusive relationship and setting goals for herself—particularly goals that would help others—profoundly impacted him. He wanted to help her now, he truly did.

He prayed that she would let him.

Monday morning found Bridget anxiously waiting for Dr. Burgess's arrival. Sawyer sat in a chair, apparently absorbed in the morning newspaper and appearing calmer than she felt, but then again he didn't have nearly as much at stake as she did.

Or did he?

His motivation for sticking around was still a puzzle to her, especially since he still hadn't made a move on buying the clinic. But she was finding it hard to hold on to any resentment. She had told him her dark secret and he had been comforting, positive and supportive. If anything, she had the distinct impression that he held her in higher esteem than he had before.

She thought about Sawyer's offer to help her draw up a business plan. She had sworn that after Wes she would never need or trust a man to help her.

Was she changing her mind about that?

Sawyer glanced up from the newspaper then and smiled encouragingly in her direction.

Maybe she was.

Maybe it was time to consider that what had happened with Wes didn't have to impact every decision she made, or her views of men, for the rest of her life.

Dr. Burgess arrived looking harried. Bridget observed that her boss paradoxically appeared both younger because of her casual dress, blue jeans and a checkered blouse but also older because of the worry lines that marred her strong-boned, striking face.

Her own concerns rushed out of Bridget as she stepped forward to greet the doctor with a spontaneous hug.

"How's your mom?" she asked, though she could already see the answer.

Sawyer put aside his newspaper and came to join them.

"Things aren't good," Dr. Burgess said tersely. Then she softened. "I do appreciate you asking. It's been hard watching her decline so quickly."

Tears glistened in the eyes of the woman who had seen so many people through so many difficult situations with their beloved pets over the years. Bridget felt an answering sting in her own eyes. Sawyer reached out and gave her shoulder a reassuring pat.

Bridget was surprised to realize that she didn't mind the gesture.

"Well, I guess we'd better get to it," Dr. Burgess said. "Grab yourselves a tea or coffee and come to my office."

Bridget's nervous stomach had no appetite for any beverage and Sawyer also declined.

As Bridget had feared, the rumor was true: Dr. Burgess was indeed prepared to sell the clinic to the sporting goods store conglomerate.

"I know that's not what you wanted to hear, Bridget," she said. "And it's not the way I wanted things to turn out but I need to be practical. My mother needs me, her care is expensive and it would be foolish for me to turn down their offer."

She turned to Sawyer. "I brought you in here to confirm that everything is okay with the accounts. I assume you would have told me by now if you'd run into anything untoward."

"Everything is fine," Sawyer said. "I can send you my report anytime."

So why hadn't he? Bridget wondered again. She thought about his whispering little girl and the ache she often saw in his eyes.

Maybe he was looking for a new start just like she was. Empathy filled her heart. But her hold on the new Bridget was tenuous and she didn't know if she wanted to understand what Sawyer was going through, not if it meant that hold unraveling and slipping through her fingers.

Beside her, Sawyer sat up straighter in his chair and leaned forward, his jaw thrust forward with purpose.

"When's the deadline date to sell?" he asked.

"Not long," Dr. Burgess said. "They want to be set up for business by November to take advantage of the Christmas season and they will need time to do renovations before then. So I can't imagine them letting it go longer than August or September."

"Can you give Bridget and I time to come up with something?" Sawyer asked.

Bridget jolted up and shot forward in her own chair, mimicking his posture, while the doctor looked puzzled.

"What do you mean 'come up with something'?" she asked.

"Yes," Bridget echoed with, her own voice distant in her ears. "What do you mean?"

If he was going to step in and outbid the other buyer, wouldn't he just do that? Why was he asking that both of them be given time to come up with something?

"Are you interested in doing something with the property, Bridget?" The doctor looked at her.

Bridget tightened her lips and raked her fingers through her hair. She was frustrated with Sawyer for putting her in this position. She hadn't wanted to say anything to her boss until she was in a position to make an offer.

It took her a moment to realize that Sawyer was answering for her. He told Dr. Burgess how hard she was working on her classes, how she believed that rescue animals and lonely or grieving people could help each other and how he was sure that with the right approach, she could convince the bank that her idea was worthy of consideration.

"And I want to help her with a business plan," Sawyer concluded.

A torrent of conflicting reactions flooded through Bridget. She pressed her hands to her warming cheeks, almost unable to believe that Sawyer not only remembered her ideas but also thought them worthy. But behind that, the part of her that still struggled to trust that any man could have her best interests at heart asked, *Why?*

"What's in it for you?" she asked tersely. "I thought you were going to make an offer on the clinic yourself."

She felt slightly guilty tossing that last comment out there, but now Dr. Burgess would be aware of everything.

Dr. Burgess leaned back in her chair, folded her arms and looked back and forth between Sawyer and Bridget.

"Well," she said. "Isn't this interesting?"

Bridget uneasily suspected that the doctor was referring to more than them both having an interest in the property.

"Is that true, Sawyer?" Dr. Burgess asked. "Were you going to make an offer on the property?"

"I mentioned the possibility when I first arrived here, yes," Sawyer said.

"But now you've changed your mind and

you'd rather help Bridget?" Dr. Burgess persisted and Bridget wondered if she was imagining that there was a twinkle in her boss's deep brown eyes.

Tension threaded through her as she waited to hear what Sawyer would say.

"My life is a bit up in the air right now," he answered, surprising her with his honesty. "I may be looking for a new opportunity but I'm not sure if it will be here in Green Valley or somewhere else. As an experienced businessman, I know a good idea when I hear one and I know how important the right property and location is to bring those kinds of ideas to fruition. I did have an interest in the property, but taking everything into account, I do believe that Bridget is the best candidate for it."

Except I can't afford it, Bridget inwardly protested, even as the thought did a stumbling dance with the realization that someone believed in her. She just hadn't expected her business rival to be that person.

God, You do have an unexpected way of answering my prayers. Please help me to know whether I can trust this answer.

"And you think you can help her achieve this goal?" Dr. Burgess asked. Her eyes were thoughtful.

"I know I can help her present the idea in

such a way that others recognize the value in it," Sawyer said.

He sounded so formal and businesslike, it wasn't until he finally glanced in her direction that she saw something else in his eyes—something that told her again that it hadn't been a mistake to open up to him and that it may not be a mistake to trust him.

"I haven't signed the contract—yet," Dr. Burgess said thoughtfully. "I suppose there would be some time. But—" she raised a cautioning finger "—not a whole lot of time. I can't afford to miss this opportunity.

"Bridget, you've been almost like a daughter to me. You've got the kindest heart I know of and you're smarter than you give yourself credit for. If Sawyer is willing to help you and you can get what you need to move forward on this, I'll postpone on signing off on the other offer as long as I can."

"Thank you," Sawyer said. "That's all we can ask for now."

"Thank you," Bridget echoed.

"Sawyer, can I have a few minutes alone with Doc B?" she asked. "I just need to talk to her about a couple of other things. That is, if you have time," she added to the doctor.

"Yes, I have a few minutes."

Sawyer excused himself.

After he was gone Bridget said, "I didn't mean for you to feel put on the spot or for you to make a decision that isn't in the best interests of you and your mother."

"That young man thinks you have what it takes," Dr. Burgess answered. "Isn't it time that you did too?"

"But what if I don't have what it takes?"

Dr. Burgess was quiet for a moment.

"We don't talk a lot about faith in a place of business," she said. "Which I sometimes think is a shame. I know you have faith and so do I, and hearing myself say that is a good reminder for me too. Sometimes there's only one way to answer a question like that and that's to dive right in. Why don't we both try to trust that God will work in our lives the way He needs to?"

Bridget pondered. She had returned to her morning devotionals and just that morning had read something in the second book of Timothy that told her that God did not give His people a spirit of fear but of courage and love and a sound mind. It was time to show evidence in her own life that she believed that.

"I can do that," she said.

Dr. Burgess nodded with satisfaction. "Then I can too."

Still, a fear lingered with Bridget. It was a fear

that was different than that of taking a chance or of fearing she could never trust someone.

It was a fear that she could come to count too much on Sawyer Blume. He was a good man. He wanted to help. But she had to know she could do this with or without him, even if her life was enhanced by his presence. She resolved to be vigilant and to do whatever she needed to do to ensure that she charted her own course.

Chapter Eleven

On Tuesday morning, Bridget and Sophie arrived early at Mildred's because Mildred had extended a breakfast invitation.

Sawyer was cautiously okay with that, though he hoped that his host wasn't getting any ideas about him and Bridget.

Yesterday had been a turning point and he was relieved that Bridget was now willing to accept his help. They'd even taken their lunch break together in the small office staff room and started talking things over.

Of course, it still didn't solve his dilemma about what his next step should be, but the sharp edges of his fear were smoothed away a bit by helping Bridget, and he was doing his best to believe there would still be an answer for both of them.

They found their places at the table, which

was heaped with a platter of pancakes and sausage, one of freshly sliced oranges and grapefruit, carafes of tea and coffee and a pitcher of orange juice.

Mildred said a prayer of thanks over the food and then encouraged them to dig in.

"You've outdone yourself, Mildred," Bridget said, drizzling syrup over her pancake. "I see a big nap in my future. Too bad it's a work morning."

"Everything looks delicious," Sawyer agreed as he cut Delilah's pancakes into bites for her.

They were all startled when Sophie's head popped out beside Delilah's plate and she tugged a pancake off of it.

Delilah squeaked, a laugh burst out of Sawyer, which he quickly silenced, and Mildred said, "Oh my!" in a tone of wonderment.

Bridget's cheeks flamed red. "I'm so embarrassed," she said. "Sophie knows I always give her any misshapen pancakes but that's no excuse." She stood up. "Sophie, come here right now!"

But the dog, pleased with the stir she had caused, frolicked and ran in circles, bobbing her head up and down so that the pancake flapped around. Anytime Bridget got anywhere close to her, Sophie would zigzag and bolt in the other direction.

Sawyer could see Bridget trying to keep her sense of humor about it, but it was battling against her growing sense of frustration and embarrassment. After what she had told him, he sensed that she would judge herself harshly in these situations. He wished he could help but didn't want to seem like he doubted her ability to handle the situation.

Mildred, probably sensing that Bridget didn't need an audience, excused herself, murmuring something about forgetting to put butter out. But Delilah watched the spectacle closely.

She turned to him and put her small hand on his arm. "Daddy," she whispered. "Play Mozart, on your phone."

Sawyer shook his head, puzzled.

"Daddy." She tugged his arm insistently.

So, he pulled out his phone and found something he sometimes played for Delilah when she was having an especially tough time.

The music swelled into the room. Bridget's head spun in its direction, her eyes showed that she, like Sawyer, was recalling their first encounter when he'd played the same tune to calm Delilah's temper. How far they'd come since that day.

But then they were both distracted by Sophie's reaction to the music and he understood what Delilah's intent had been.

Sophie whined softly, tilting her head to the side. She released her hold on the pancake and flopped to the ground resting her head on her paws.

"Did you see that?" Bridget asked Sawyer. "It's like what you did for Delilah when I first met you."

"It was Delilah's idea," Sawyer confirmed.

Bridget returned to the table with another apology, which the others graciously brushed off.

"It's a good thing you got an early start, though," Mildred said, after returning to the table with the butter. "You still have time to enjoy some breakfast."

But Bridget didn't resume eating right away. She was thinking hard about something.

"When I first met you," she said to Sawyer, "you told me you'd always been interested in music but you'd never done anything with it. But you know what it does for Delilah and you saw what it did for Sophie just now..."

She shook her head. "Never mind, I'm just thinking."

But, without her saying anything more, Sawyer caught the seed of the idea she had planted—figuring out how music could work into the kind of work she wanted to do—and silently, prayerfully began to water it.

Could it be possible that God would find a way to return something he'd always loved back into his life in a meaningful way? Only time would tell, but he couldn't remember the last time he felt the door so wide-open to hope.

Now as they finished up their breakfast, Mildred said, "You know there's a jazz concert at the community center on Friday night."

"I did hear that," Sawyer acknowledged.

"Bridget likes music too," Mildred added.

Ahh, about as subtle as a sledgehammer.

He would have found a way to change the subject, especially seeing the way Bridget's face wavered between amusement and wariness, but then Delilah whispered, "Sophie and me love music," and bounced happily in her chair.

Besides, he didn't want to push his craving for music aside, not after what he and Bridget had witnessed and the ideas it stirred in both of them.

He couldn't ignore the pleasure he felt at being on the same page with her.

"Would you like to see the concert, Dee-Dee?" he asked her.

She nodded enthusiastically.

Of course Bridget didn't want to go on a date; he knew that. She still had emotional wounds that ran deep.

"Delilah and I would be pleased if you would

join us, Bridget," he said, careful to emphasize that it didn't have to be anything more than the three of them hanging out together.

He couldn't deny his happiness when she answered in a calm, sure voice. "I'd like that."

What should he wear on an outing that wasn't a date? Sawyer wondered on Friday night, and why did he have to keep reminding himself that it wasn't a date?

"Ready to go, Daddy?" Delilah whispered and tugged on his sleeve. Sawyer smiled down at her. She was wearing a denim jumper over a pink blouse and Mildred had coaxed her hair into two tidy braids.

"You look very pretty," he told her. "I'd better hurry up and get changed so I look as nice as you do."

He went to his room and hurriedly pulled on a clean pair of blue jeans and a dark blue shirt that Tina had always told him brought out his eyes. But thinking about Tina made attending the concert with another woman feel like a betrayal, so he shoved the thought aside.

Still, he hoped that Bridget would like the shirt.

They had agreed they would just meet at the community hall.

"My lady." Sawyer offered Delilah his arm. She giggled as she looped her arm through his.

"Are you sure you won't change your mind about joining us, Mildred?" Sawyer asked.

"Oh, bless you, no." Mildred kept a careful eye on oil that was heating on the stove for her popcorn. There would be no microwave popcorn for her. "I'm content to have some quiet time. You go ahead and enjoy yourselves… And Sawyer?"

He turned back. "Yes?"

"Just let the evening be whatever it turns out to be."

Puzzling over Mildred's remark, Sawyer was distracted as they began their walk to the hall.

The community hall buzzed with activity, the noise of chatter and the distant sound of instruments being tuned. Sawyer scanned the room for Bridget and didn't see her but waved at Seth and Rena Acoose.

"I don't see Ms. Connelly, do you?" he asked Delilah.

"I'm here," Bridget said.

Sawyer turned in the direction of her voice and the sight of her took his breath away.

She wore a turquoise blue dress with a lacy knit, cream-colored shawl draped around her shoulders. The color of the dress made her eyes an even more stunning shade of blue.

"You look beautiful," Delilah said in a wistful, whispering voice that turned Sawyer's heart over as he heard his daughter say the words he wanted to say.

"Delilah's absolutely right," he said instead, keeping his tone light. He didn't want to do anything at all to make Bridget uncomfortable.

But she smiled at Delilah and said, "You look very beautiful too." She gently straightened the ribbon on one of Delilah's braids.

"Do you think my daddy looks nice too?" Delilah asked.

"Yes, your daddy looks nice," Bridget said.

"You match," Delilah added.

Their eyes met over her head. Sawyer grinned encouragingly at Bridget and she smiled back.

"You really do look beautiful," he told her as they started to move with the crowd into the hall. Her smile faltered a bit but her eyes glowed.

They found good seats only a few rows from the front. Sawyer asked Delilah if she needed to use the restroom before the concert started, as they were hemmed in the middle of a row, but she shook her head no.

"I can take her out if she needs to go later," Bridget said.

"It's a good thing we came when we did,"

Sawyer remarked, looking around the crowd. "It's filling up quickly in here."

Delilah sat between him and Bridget, but even so he was wholly aware of Bridget's presence.

"Hi, Bridge," Rena Acoose said from the seat on the other side of Bridget.

Both Seth and Rena sang in the church choir at Green Valley Community Church and appreciated good music, he'd been told.

"How did you manage to get away from the café for the evening?" Bridget asked.

"Eugenie is running the show at the café," Seth said. "And she's got me on speed dial. Besides—" he looked around "—judging by how this place is filling up, I don't think we'll be busy until later."

The lights dimmed and the buzzing crowd slowly subsided into silence.

The jazz trio entered and took their bows to applause. As the first haunting notes of the saxophone began to tell its plaintive tale, Delilah jiggled her father's arm and whispered, "Daddy, trade me places. The lady in front of me has big hair."

Sawyer obliged and when he took the seat beside Bridget, his arm brushed hers on the armrest.

"Sorry," they said in unison, each pulling their arms away.

But, as the music overtook them, they both relaxed and Sawyer found himself enjoying Bridget's close proximity, the appealing scent of her lightly perfumed soap and apple-scented shampoo and, especially, the way she became so completely absorbed in the music that she no longer jerked away when their arms touched.

The concert wasn't long so there was no intermission. The musicians played straight through, keeping the hypnotic spell of the music going, carrying the deepest human emotions in the slide of the trombone and the sigh of the clarinet. All too soon, though, the music ended and the lights came back up.

Sawyer realized that Bridget was nestled into him and his arm was resting along the back of her chair. He turned to her and they locked eyes and the buzzing crowd seemed to fade away like they didn't exist.

He realized that he would do anything he could to help and protect her.

But then, like she was pulling herself out of a dream, Bridget shook her head and made herself busy retrieving her purse and smoothing non-existent wrinkles out of her dress.

"How did you like that, Dee-Dee?" Sawyer turned his attention to his daughter while Bridget recovered herself and asked Rena and Seth if they'd enjoyed the concert.

"It was great," Rena said as Seth checked his phone messages.

"Eugenie says that things are picking up at the café," he remarked. "I guess I'd better head that way. Why don't the three of you stop by for an after-show treat on me?"

The three of you...

Sawyer looked questioningly in Bridget's direction.

"That's a really nice offer, Seth," Bridget said. "Maybe we'll do that."

"Great!" Seth said. "Maybe see you there." He began to make his way down the aisle chatting with people along the way.

"At this rate, he'll never get there," Rena said with amused affection. She leaned closer to Bridget and said something that Sawyer couldn't hear, but it caused a slightly troubled expression to cross Bridget's face before she gave what he suspected was an insincere chuckle.

He wondered what Rena, who was undoubtedly a kind and sensitive woman, could have said to Bridget to unnerve her.

Bridget couldn't get her legs to move; Rena's words that it was good to see her acting like her old self had frozen her to the spot. Rena had meant her statement as a positive thing because she didn't know that Bridget didn't *want* to be her old self. Her old self trusted too easily and invited disrespect. She could not—absolutely would not—be that person again.

It was too bad because the evening had been about as close to perfect as any she could remember, but she could never allow it to happen again. She'd acted like she was on a date with Sawyer, snuggling into him, his arm practically around her.

And if Rena had noticed, what conclusions must Sawyer himself be coming to? She needed to set it straight.

"I don't think it's such a great idea that we go to Seth's together," she said, when they were outside.

Sawyer appeared resigned, like he had been expecting something of the sort, but he asked, "Why's that?"

"Because I don't want anyone to assume that we're dating," she answered bluntly.

"How about this?" he said after a brief pause. "We go and talk about that whole music thing and how it impacted Sophie and then we'll be two people, with a chaperone—" he nodded in Delilah's direction "—talking over some new strategies for your program and most definitely not on a date. How does that sound?"

The idea of discussing the fledgling idea further did intrigue Bridget, so she said, "Actually, that sounds good."

When she saw the smile that lit Sawyer's face and saw the way Delilah jumped up and down and clapped her hands when her dad told her the plan, she knew she would have been disappointed if she'd decided to end the evening then and there.

Since Wes, she'd already had so many nights alone with her own thoughts. At first, she appreciated the barrier of safety between her and the outside world, but she was beginning to think more about what she could be missing.

"If you can go ahead and get a table," she said, "I want to take Sophie for a quick walk and then I'll join you."

They agreed and as she headed home to let Sophie out, her steps and her heart were light with anticipation.

"So, you like the classics, do you?" she said to the dog as she fastened on her leash.

Sophie demurely rolled her eyes.

"You and Delilah might just have helped me with something," Bridget told her, and Sophie yipped in reply, anticipating her walk.

Bridget briefly considered changing into something more casual before heading to Seth's, but she couldn't get Sawyer's compliment out of her mind. There was nothing wrong with wanting to feel pretty, she told herself, even if it was for a business meeting of sorts.

When Bridget got to the café it was teeming with the after-concert crowd, eager for refreshment. She waved at and greeted several people she knew, while her eyes scanned the room, hoping that Sawyer had managed to secure seats for them.

"Bridget!" Seth called out and waved her over. "I made sure your date got a good table."

His words slammed the brakes on Bridget's go-with-the-flow attitude for a moment. Rena must have said something to him.

"It's not a date," she explained. "We're working together right now and we're friends." As she said it she realized the latter was the truth, and also realized that she didn't really have to explain. People were going to think what they wanted.

It was okay for her to enjoy herself.

She couldn't wait to share this epiphany with the women in the support group. She was making progress.

But she also hoped to convey the same to Sawyer.

"I'm glad you made it." Sawyer greeted her.

"Me too," Bridget said. Delilah sat across the table from her dad and Bridget chose to take the empty seat beside her. It wasn't that it hadn't been lovely to sit beside Sawyer at the concert. His firm but comforting physique, his fresh-laundry smell, his attentiveness to the music, all combined to provide a feeling of safety.

But that wasn't the only sensation she experienced sitting close to him. No, if she was being honest, she was out-and-out attracted to him.

There was still no guarantee that he was going to be around for any length of time, though, and, even if he was, she didn't want to lose sight of the promise she'd made to herself not to let any man make her doubt her own strengths. No matter what Sawyer decided, it was ultimately up to her to meet the goals she'd set for herself.

Eugenie stopped by their table and they decided to order a plate of onion rings to share and three colas.

While they waited for Eugenie to bring the food, Charlotte appeared at their table with Tyson in tow.

"Would Delilah like to come sit with us?" Charlotte asked.

"C'mon, it'll be fun," Tyson urged.

Delilah looked at her dad, asking with wide eyes and a big smile.

"Sure," Sawyer agreed. "I'll ask Eugenie to send your drink over and some of the onion rings."

Bridget's stomach was in a not-unpleasant

jumble when he said to her after the others had left, "Besides, it will give us a chance to talk."

It took her a minute to remember that they'd said they were going to talk about Sophie's reaction to the music and what it could mean for her work going forward, and she was glad to have a chance to regroup when Eugenie delivered their food.

They took a moment to savor a couple of the sweet onions encased in the lightly crispy batter, followed by sips of the ice-cold cola.

Bridget dabbed her mouth with a napkin.

"How do you think Delilah knew to try the music with Sophie?" she asked.

Sawyer smiled and shrugged. "She's a smart little girl. She pays attention to things."

"If we were…" Bridget stopped and corrected herself. "If I was to make this part of the program, I wonder how I'd go about it. How would I make sure it wasn't just a fluke?"

A flicker of something through Sawyer's eyes told her that he had noticed the change she had made from "we" to "I." She fought the urge to apologize. Yes, Sawyer was attractive and yes, she liked him and even trusted him. But she was still reluctant to count on anyone but herself.

But it was getting harder to remember that after she had shared her secret with him, and with the way his eyes focused on her from across the table.

Sawyer seemed to consider saying something, then straightened in his chair, pushed his glasses up his nose and with those two gestures turned back into a businessman.

"You could set up a study," he suggested. "Ask for test cases. See if anyone has a pet with behavioral problems or anxiety and see what hearing the music does for them."

"But where would I do all of that?" Bridget fretted. "No matter how I look at this, I'm back to square one. The clinic is the ideal place for everything I want to do. But…" Her voice trailed off.

She didn't want this evening to slide into a self-pity party. She didn't want Sawyer to know that she *had* self-pity parties.

"Bridget." Sawyer's businesslike tone had softened and she didn't know whether that made things better or worse. She decided the latter because she already had so much to think about without being confused over emotions she wasn't prepared to entertain.

"I have the money to invest in the clinic," Sawyer said. "Or I could cosign a loan for you at the bank. I have the collateral to back it up. I could help you make this happen."

Bridget shook her head, automatically rejecting the idea. "No, absolutely not."

"Why not?" Sawyer asked, not accusingly, but like he genuinely wanted to understand.

A thousand reasons crowded into Bridget's mind, but before she could pluck out the one that she could best put words to, Eugenie stopped by their table to ask if they needed anything else and Sawyer took the interlude as an opportunity to wave in Delilah's direction and make sure she was doing okay.

But the reprieve was over all too quickly and Sawyer still wanted an answer.

"Because this is my project," she said, lifting her chin. "And it's my problem to figure out. Besides, I don't get what's changed with you. You wanted the property for yourself and now you want to give it to me."

"Not give," Sawyer corrected. "This would be a business deal and I never get involved in a business deal unless I think it has real potential."

"But you wanted the property to set up your *own* business," she persisted.

"I thought I did," Sawyer acknowledged. He grew quiet for a moment and rubbed his palm against the side of his face. When he looked up at her, she saw again the weariness in his eyes.

"Things change," he said. "The truth is, I don't know exactly what my next step is." He briefly recounted how he had been dismissed from the big project he'd been working on with the family business.

"I'm sorry to hear that," Bridget said. But her stomach still churned with uncertainty. So he'd had a falling-out with his father. She didn't want to be anyone's backup plan. She couldn't afford to be, financially or, especially not, emotionally.

"That's okay," Sawyer said. "In some ways it's good that the pressure is off on that end. I've been thinking about a change for Delilah and me for a while now and honestly, with my background, I can always get work somewhere. I just want… I want to be involved in something meaningful."

"I guess… I guess I can understand that," Bridget said softly. She contemplatively ate another onion ring, slowly chewing. Sweet onion and salty batter mingled on her tongue.

"Hi, Bridget." Tyson was at their table with Delilah in tow. "Mr. Blume?" he said. "Can I take Delilah to show her the rows of all the jams and jellies that Seth and Rena make? Seth said it was okay."

Sawyer glanced at his watch. "Sure," he said. "Go ahead."

Bridget watched him watch his little girl. She knew he would do anything for her, and Delilah and Sophie did have a special bond.

"You really believe this could work?" she asked.

"We'd have to do some trial runs," Sawyer said, turning his attention back to her. "To see if there are consistent-enough responses to the music, what kind of music and all that. But, yes, I definitely think there's something there.

"Besides," he added. "I'm going to play my last card here. You know that Dr. Burgess is running on a deadline. She already has an offer and the only thing stopping her from snatching it up is that she loves you and believes in you. But she's not going to wait forever and I sincerely believe I'm your best option at this point. I get that it wouldn't feel right to you to accept a loan directly from me. But I could help you with the bank."

Countless questions whirled through Bridget's head. She did her best to gather them into a prayer.

She found an answer in Sawyer's steady gaze. There was nothing hidden in the clear light of his eyes, no hidden agenda. There wasn't really any arguing with what he had said.

"This is my program," she said, wanting to be clear. "I don't want to take your financial backing if it means that you try to dominate things or force your ideas on me. I refuse to be in a relationship like that again, business or otherwise. And, one way or another, I will pay back every penny of that loan."

"I wouldn't have it any other way," Sawyer said. "Bridget, please understand, I'm not offering to do this because I think you're incapable or because I feel sorry for you, or anything like that. I'm doing it because I know you are strong and capable and because I know this thing could really have legs."

"Four legs?" Bridget couldn't resist.

When Sawyer grinned back, a feeling of anticipation overcame her, mingled with the cautionary note that it was just business.

The problem was that Sawyer's appealing looks and, more importantly, the respect he showed her, made her question if that was all she wanted.

Chapter Twelve

Sunday morning came and Sawyer woke up with an unexpected but undeniable urge to attend church. He couldn't help thinking that God had a hand in opening Bridget's heart and mind to let him assist her, and he was grateful. Maybe it was time to explore that gratitude a little further.

If only he could stop wanting to explore another connection a little further. He truly did believe that there was something there with the music and people and their pets, and he knew he was confident he could convince the bank it was worthy of investment, if Bridget continued to refuse his own offer to invest, which he suspected she would.

But was being Bridget's partner in business all he really wanted?

In little flashes throughout the weekend,

memories of the brush of her soft, warm arm and the subtle scent of the apple-scented shampoo she used kept jarring him out of whatever he was doing.

But he reluctantly answered his own question: being her business partner was all he *could* want. Even if Bridget was willing, which she definitely wasn't, it wasn't fair to bring the complicated grief that he and Delilah were still coping with into her life.

Sawyer looked into the half-open door of Delilah's room. She was sitting cross-legged on the braided rug on the polished hardwood floor. He recognized the tune she hummed as one of the pieces they'd heard on Friday night, as she sorted through a box of colored beads that Mildred found for her. Mildred was going to teach her how to make jewelry.

She was still in her pajamas—not pink for a change—but blue ones with a sleeveless top and the bottoms that reminded Sawyer of Bermuda shorts. They were adorned with pictures of wide-eyed fluffy white dogs.

His daughter looked comfortable in her environment, as she carefully studied and sorted each bead.

"Morning, Dee-Dee," he said.

Delilah looked up and smiled at him.

"I'm thinking about going to church this

morning, the same place that we went to where you heard stories and made crafts and played with Tyson and Max and Michael."

A cautiously interested expression crept across her face.

"Would you like to go to church with me?" Sawyer asked.

Delilah considered and asked, "Do I have to go to the Sunday school if I don't want to?"

"You don't have to do anything you don't want to do, but we can see how you feel when we get there. Does that sound fair?"

Delilah nodded.

"But you're not going to go in your pj's, are you? Or maybe I should go and put mine back on and people might think we're twins."

She rolled her eyes at him.

Sawyer left her to change and went downstairs to tell Mildred of their plans.

"How nice," she said. "We can walk over there together. I expect we'll see Bridget there."

"Probably," Sawyer agreed. A silence stretched between them that made him wonder why Mildred had chosen to mention it.

"Delilah's just getting dressed," he said, to break the silence and change the subject.

"That's fine," Mildred said. "We have plenty of time."

Then, unable to resist, Sawyer asked, "Did

you ever babysit Bridget when she was a little girl?"

"Yes, I sure did," Mildred said, settling back comfortably in her kitchen chair like she was about to embark on a long story.

Sawyer took his own chair. "What was she like?"

Mildred's eyes twinkled at him. "Very much like the person you see today," she said. "Pretty, kind, full of fun, always with some idea or another up her sleeve. She always liked to have fun, our Bridget. She likes being around people and people love her."

Our Bridget.

"Does she seem any different to you these days?" Sawyer didn't know exactly what he hoped to glean from Mildred and he treaded carefully so as not to expose the secret that Bridget had entrusted to him. But he had an irresistible desire to know more about her.

Mildred pondered as she dipped a tea bag into her cup and pulled it back out again. "Well, I think she's more grown-up now," she mused. "And I think that growing up comes with some hard lessons."

Sawyer suddenly sensed that Mildred wasn't completely unaware of the situation, but, like him, was choosing not to be indiscreet.

She looked pointedly at him. "It would be

lovely if she could be reminded that there are many people—perhaps a nice young man like yourself—who have her best interests at heart."

He was saved from having to answer when Delilah came into the kitchen wearing the same dress she had worn to Friday night's concert and a baseball cap over her messy hair.

"Delilah, would you like braids for church?" Mildred suggested.

"Oh, I don't know," Sawyer said, grinning fondly as his heart brimmed at seeing a glimpse of his spunky, live-life-her-way daughter. "I kind of like the look myself."

Delilah grinned too and spun the cap around backward.

Mildred shook her head but with a smile.

A little while later, almost as soon as they entered Green Valley Community Church, Tyson spotted them and convinced Delilah that it would be a great idea for her to join him in the Sunday school class downstairs.

"You sit with your dad at the start," he explained. "There's gonna be a song, then announcements, which is like the ladies are selling baking or they want someone to cut the grass. Then Pastor calls us up for a story—you can sit by me—and then we go downstairs where, believe me, it's a lot more fun."

Sawyer was happy that Delilah agreed to go

to Sunday school with Tyson, but when she left, memories assaulted him of Tina and himself, with a younger Delilah, sitting in a pew. He had believed in so much then: in the saving power of God, in the sanctity of a marriage he didn't know would be forced to an end so soon.

Panic tightened his chest and he fought the urge to bolt out of the church. He sat at the end of the pew and Mildred sat beside him. He didn't want to alarm her or draw attention to himself, so he made himself breathe slowly in and out and stared at the program until the swimming words came into focus.

When his chest stopped stuttering, Sawyer took a moment to scan the congregation, instinctively searching for Bridget. He was in the back, and most of the other attendees were already seated when they'd come in, and she wouldn't have seen him arrive or known to look for him. He spotted her just as the worship music swelled to joyously greet the morning and the congregation rose in response. She was standing between an older man and woman, who he assumed were her parents. She wore a white-and-purple-flowered sundress with a mauve open-knit shawl and her pretty blond hair spilled down her back like a waterfall of sunbeams.

The sight of her had the paradoxical impact of comforting and unsettling him.

Sawyer wasn't sure if he would be able to concentrate on the sermon but the words the pastor spoke about carrying the burden of secrets caught his attention and he thought again about how Bridget had trusted him with hers.

Was that the real reason he wanted to help Bridget out with her finances, despite what he had told her? Was he still trying to prove to himself that it wasn't too late to save someone? "So how did you like that?" Mildred asked him when the notes of the final worship song had faded away.

"I enjoyed it," Sawyer said, his other thoughts too complicated to put into words.

"The pastor is a good speaker," Mildred said. "He always manages to get right to the heart of matters. Would you like to meet some more people?"

"I could do that," Sawyer agreed. "But I want to check in with Delilah first." He didn't add that he hoped to run into Bridget too as he weaved his way through the chattering clusters in the main hall.

But when she saw him and hurried over, her welcoming smile warmed him.

"It's great you came," she said. "Did you enjoy it?" She looked around. "Where's Delilah?"

"Tyson talked her into Sunday school," Sawyer explained. "And, yes, the sermon and music were great. I'm on my way to get Delilah now. Come with me, I know she'd love to see you."

When they got downstairs, the hallways were filled with children chatting and laughing and showing off their crafts and pictures.

Tyson saw them before Delilah did and ran toward them, bringing Delilah along by the hand.

Sawyer was relieved to see that she looked happy.

"Did you have fun, Dee-Dee?" he asked her.

Delilah nodded vigorously.

"We talked about Moses and the Ten Commandments today," Tyson said. "Hey, there's my mom and dad!" He made a beeline for Paul and Charlotte.

Charlotte waved the rest of them over.

"Want to join us for Sunday brunch?" she invited. "Our parents have gone ahead to save a table. You know how lined up it gets for Seth's brunch—Saskatoon berry pancakes, sausage and bacon, fluffy scrambled eggs and cheesy omelets. You know you want to." She smiled teasingly.

"We'd love to come," Sawyer said, then realized he'd spoken for all of them and glanced at Bridget.

She hesitated but only momentarily. "Sure, sounds fun."

"You can sit by me," Tyson told Delilah. "I can show you what's best for brunch. I'm pretty much a regular, so I know those kinds of things."

"That's good of you, Ty." Bridget smiled.

When they arrived at the café, the couple who Bridget had been with at church waved them over to a table where they sat with another older couple, who Sawyer guessed must be Charlotte's parents.

Bridget introduced them, saying only, "This is Sawyer Blume. He's been doing the audit at the clinic. And this is his daughter, Delilah. These are my parents."

They shook hands and Sawyer couldn't miss the way Bridget's mother's eyes lit up with curiosity, no doubt wondering why the vet's auditor was joining them for brunch.

"Good to see you, sweetheart," Bridget's father said. "Happy you could join us."

"Finally," her mother added. Sawyer watched Bridget's face tighten, but she managed to keep her smile intact.

There was a small flurry of activity as everyone sought chairs. Sawyer found himself in the middle of Bridget and Delilah.

"Paul, will you please say the blessing for us?" Charlotte asked.

"Happy to," Paul said, bowing his head.

"Dear Lord, thank you for the opportunity to share food together with family and with new friends. Help us to always remember your gifts to us and everything you do for us, each and every day. We ask this in Jesus's name. Amen."

New friends echoed through Sawyer's mind as he said "Amen" along with the others.

Sitting beside Bridget while Paul united the family in prayer was a strangely intimate experience.

As he had promised, Tyson escorted Delilah to the buffet line. Sawyer immediately sat up straighter in his chair, straining his neck to see where they were going.

"We'll be right behind them," Bridget reassured him, sliding out her chair. "And even if we weren't, there's got to be at least half a dozen people here who would keep an eye on them and be there in a split second if needed."

"I guess I'm still not used to small towns," Sawyer said.

"I wasn't either," Paul remarked. "But trust me, soon you won't be able to imagine living anywhere else."

Their exchange caught Charlotte's attention. "Are you planning to be around longer than you thought, Sawyer?"

He might as well say the words out loud, Sawyer thought, and solidify his commitment.

"Well, as it turns out, yes. It so happens I'm in a position to help Bridget with…"

"Who's starved besides me?" Bridget's voice was a little louder than it needed to be as she caught his eye with an expression that clearly said he wasn't to say anything more about that particular conversation.

"With…another account ledger she came across," he finished awkwardly.

Charlotte looked back and forth between them with a skeptical expression, but, to Sawyer's relief, Tyson called for her to hurry up.

But he couldn't help wondering just how many secrets Bridget intended him to keep for her, and why she didn't want her family to know about her goals.

Not that he was in any position to judge. His own family dynamics were not exactly stellar at the moment.

Soon they were all back at the table, teasing one another about the generous size of the portions of food and discussing the sermon. After a little while, the conversations split off into smaller segments.

Bridget enjoyed the food and basked in the conversations around her, but she wasn't unaware of the fact that Sawyer had been puzzled by her reaction. Sometimes she didn't know herself why it wasn't easy to share her hopes and dreams with her family, except that she was constantly afraid of disappointing them.

Then she gave herself a reminder from her support group: be present in the moment and appreciate it for what it is. At this moment, she was enjoying a delicious brunch and she was surrounded by people she cared about.

And, yes, Sawyer and Delilah were unarguably among those people.

Bridget leaned around Sawyer to ask Delilah, "How's your food? Are you having fun?"

Delilah nodded and smiled with her teeth stained with berries.

Bridget noticed that she was carefully setting aside bites of pancake that didn't have any butter or syrup on them. "Let me guess," she said. "You're saving those for Sophie?"

The little girl nodded.

Sawyer cut Delilah's piece of ham up for her and then, with the others absorbed in conversation, turned to Bridget and said in a low voice, "I'm sorry about earlier. I didn't know you didn't want me to say anything."

A wave of all-too-familiar guilt rocked through Bridget's stomach. She didn't want to get her family's hopes up and disappoint them, but she didn't want Sawyer to feel like he had done something wrong either. Would there ever come a time in her life when she wasn't walking a barb-wired fence, trying to please people while not losing herself in the process?

"It's okay," she said. "I'll tell you more about it later." She wasn't sure why she had added the latter part—her instinct was never to open up more than she had to—but something about Sawyer's way of listening without commentary made it easy to talk to him.

Before they could continue any kind of conversation, though, Lenore Connelly turned her attention on Sawyer and began to ask him questions about his work and his family.

Apprehension darted through Bridget as the questions hurtled toward the inevitable end of putting Sawyer in an awkward spot. Her aunt Lenore wasn't exactly known for her subtlety and had already made some probing comments about what a quiet little girl Delilah was.

Without giving herself time to rethink it, her hand shot out toward her glass of water, toppling it and sending a small pool spreading out across the table.

While Seth, whose eyes were everywhere, ran forward with a cloth and the others sprang into action to help, Sawyer briefly squeezed her hand under the table sending warmth through her.

"I know what you did." His low voice warmed her even more. "Thank you."

* * *

After supper on Monday, Bridget and Sophie headed toward the park to meet Sawyer and Delilah. The meeting had several purposes: it would give Sophie and Delilah a chance to see each other and it would be another opportunity to check out Sophie's response to the music—whether it was just a fluke or not—and, with the hope that it wasn't a fluke, start nailing down what Bridget's new business plan would look like.

It was a perfect evening for time in the park. The sun still provided enough light and warmth but there was a cooling breeze as well.

Bridget's heart hitched when she saw the two of them. Much as she tried to steel herself against it, they had become an important part of her life. She took a chance and let Sophie off her leash to bound toward them, needing to distract herself from emotions she wasn't ready to deal with.

"I didn't really get a chance to talk to you after brunch yesterday," she said, when she had caught up with them. "My aunt Lenore means well but she isn't exactly known for her tact."

"That's okay," Sawyer said. "It's natural for them to be curious about me, no need to apologize. Although—" his grin sent a pleasant shock through her "—I did enjoy the water trick."

Bridget blushed and laughed. "It was the best I could do on short notice."

She looked in the direction of Delilah and Sophie, who were practicing the shake-a-paw trick.

"Should we give the music a try?" Sawyer asked.

Bridget considered, then slowly shook her head. "Let them play longer."

The truth was that she enjoyed time chatting with Sawyer and, despite her best efforts not to let it get personal, she too wanted to know more about his past, not just for the sake of being curious, but because she had grown to care for him and Delilah.

She slid a glance in his direction. He looked at peace watching his daughter. Maybe now wasn't a good time to ask.

He must have sensed her gaze because he turned his eyes in her direction. His held something questioning and warm.

Or maybe it was the best time.

"Sawyer, it's not my place to ask," Bridget began hesitantly, "but…your wife… I mean, if you ever want to talk about her—I'm here."

He averted his gaze and she saw his shoulders stiffen as he angled himself away from her, and for a moment she was afraid not only that she had shut down any possibility of that conversation, but also any growing closeness and trust they'd built between them.

But then he turned back to her.

"Tina and I dated in high school," he said. "She helped me with my homework in grade ten English class and I was a goner."

He slid his gaze over in Bridget's direction again and she could tell he was gauging her reaction. She nodded her encouragement for him to continue.

"Now you've got to understand that I'm not bragging," he continued. "I'm just telling it like it is—was."

"I know," Bridget said. "I want to hear it, Sawyer."

"We were the couple that everyone looked up to," Sawyer said. "We both got good grades, for the most part, and we were involved in a lot of activities, but we complemented each other. I was ambitious and I always knew I'd go into the family business after I got my university degree and— Well, I don't want to say that Tina wasn't ambitious because she worked hard at school and she liked to be involved in things and help people—like you do. But what she wanted most was to be a good wife and mother and to have a nice home." He paused and massaged the top of his head with his fingertips. "I know that's probably making her sound—I don't know— *less* than the person she was."

"It doesn't," Bridget said. "Those are honorable things to want in life."

She swallowed an ache of sadness as she thought about how much she had wanted the same, and said, "Thank you for sharing that with me."

Sawyer looked like there was more that he wanted to say but instead he called out to Delilah and made exaggerated hand gestures to show that he was applauding her efforts.

Delilah gave a jaunty thumbs-up sign, then waggled her finger at Sophie, who did a slouching walk in a circle around her.

"Should we let them play just a little while longer?" Bridget asked while wondering if Sawyer would reveal anything else about his late wife.

She also wondered why it was important to her that he did.

"I suppose it wouldn't hurt," Sawyer answered.

They sat on the bench and Sophie lunged over to greet them like she hadn't seen them for days, before loping off again to join Delilah.

Then, into the following silence, Bridget asked. "What did she look like?"

Sawyer turned and, instead of answering right away, he studied her face.

"We don't have to talk anymore about her if you don't want," Bridget said uneasily.

Sawyer averted his eyes. "No, that's fine," he said. "I don't mind you asking. I was just trying to think of how to describe her. She's... She was, I mean, she was pretty. She had short brown hair. She was fussy about the way it was cut. She liked stylish clothes. She was always put together." He shook his head.

"Words are hard," he said. "Words don't do anyone justice."

Bridget nodded her understanding and gave Sawyer's hand a gentle squeeze.

They sat in comfortable silence, still holding hands.

Then the clearing of a throat made them both look up. Delilah and Sophie stood staring at them. Both of them had their heads tilted sideways in curiosity.

Bridget instantly dropped Sawyer's hand and offered a silent prayer that they hadn't caused the grieving little girl even more confusion. Delilah didn't look troubled, though, so much as puzzled and like she was waiting for some kind of explanation.

Bridget thought that she too could use an explanation as to exactly what was going on between her and Sawyer Blume. It wasn't just business anymore, yet it couldn't really be anything else. Even a friendship had a fast-approaching expiration date.

Dear Lord, she prayed. *Please calm my heart and help me to maintain my focus. Help me not to slip into old habits. I want to stay strong and independent.*

"If you think Delilah has had enough time to play," she said, "maybe we should get started."

Sawyer darted a look at her that she couldn't quite read.

But he said, "Yes, we probably should. Then he added, "Thank you…for asking about Tina. It's been a while since I've talked about her other than to say 'It's okay' when people tell me how sorry they are."

"You're welcome, anytime you need to talk…"

Sawyer shook his head. "I appreciate that, but there really isn't any more I want to say."

A shadow came over his face marring the summer evening and Bridget couldn't help but think that there was so much more to the story.

She couldn't help wondering, but understood what it was like to have things in your life that you just couldn't share with others. She didn't know how or why, but she strongly sensed there was more to the story about his wife's death, but just because she had trusted him with her secret didn't mean that he had to trust her with his. She was sure the knot of sadness in her would unravel itself as soon as they got down to work.

Chapter Thirteen

After their session in the park, there was no doubt that music had a significant impact on Sophie, so the next step was to see if it worked on other pets as well, which included diving into research that was already available on the impact that music could have on animals.

Except that the push-and-pull thing that she and Sawyer had going made Bridget second-guess herself as to whether letting him get involved in the project on any level was the best thing for her. Because she didn't like the way her heart deflated when he emotionally pulled back from her again after taking a step forward.

Frustrated, she scooped her cascading hair into a ponytail, glad that she was scheduled to be with the kids that particular Sunday morning so she could keep her inner turmoil to herself, assuming, of course, that Sawyer even planned to be at church…or that he cared one iota about her inner turmoil.

Seeing Delilah's wide smile when she came into the Sunday school room and saw Bridget was like being basked in warm sunshine. But that almost made matters worse.

Bridget kept herself busy when the service had ended cleaning up books and crafts and managed to be involved in a conversation with another parent when Sawyer came to pick up Delilah.

She sensed his eyes on her and glanced over and gave a casual wave, proud of herself for pulling it off when all she wanted to do was hide from him.

She knew that time didn't stand still, but never was this so apparent as it was right now. Dr. Burgess couldn't wait forever for her decision and, when Bridget thought about that, the easiest and best thing to do would be to let Sawyer get—or stay—involved, especially when she didn't have another solution.

But when she saw his eyes, even in the time it took to give a brief wave, and the way he seemed already to understand so much about her, it wasn't simple at all.

She couldn't let him know her, or think that he knew her, when he was still mostly closed down. But did she really want him to open up to her? And, if she did, why did she?

It was all so confusing and all Bridget knew was that she refused to play on an uneven playing field. She'd had more than enough of that to last a lifetime.

Monday morning brought more pressures with it. There was that mixture of relief and regret that Sawyer no longer had to come into the office on a daily basis, but that raised questions in Bridget's mind about why exactly he was sticking around.

The thought that he was waiting for an opportunity to help her caused Bridget's insides to tie in knots. But she sensed that wasn't the entire story; it seemed sometimes that he wanted to stay *away* from something as much as he wanted to stay here, and that was no way to have a relationship.

Not that they were having one.

She couldn't help wondering what Sawyer was up to now that his work at the vet was wrapped up. Of course, there was Delilah, whose whispers raised a slew of other questions about what else it was that Sawyer wouldn't talk about.

She was sure that Green Valley had something to offer them both, if only they could see it. But whether they did or not had nothing to do with her.

Dr. Burgess, on the other hand, was now a frequent presence in the office: a worried shadow of the caring and competent veterinarian she had been, as she struggled to cross that line between ending a career she loved and stepping into a completely different kind of caretaking role.

Bridget had always loved working with Doc B, but her anxious demeanor did nothing for Bridget's own anxiety and her presence was a constant reminder that the deadline loomed for her to make a decision about whether she could or could not take over the clinic and bring her own dreams to fruition.

By the time the Tuesday-night support group meeting rolled around, Bridget knew it was just what she needed.

The group met in a meeting room in the elementary school where her cousin Charlotte was a teacher. The room was plain but serviceable with a big table, plenty of chairs and a coffeepot and supplies ready to go. Many of the women could be counted on to bring baked goods or snacks for the group. Bridget wasn't much of a baker herself but sometimes eased her conscience by stopping into Seth's to pick up a batch of cookies or muffins to contribute.

Bridget always tried to arrive early enough to help set up and put the coffee on, but as usual one or two women were always ahead of her.

"Haven't started the coffee yet," Mavis said, pointing in the direction of a sink. "I see you brought cookies. Thanks. If you don't mind, try one of mine and tell Michael you like them. He helped make them."

"I will," Bridget promised. "I'm sure I will like them."

Her heart swelled at tough, practical Mavis's unquestionable love for her son, who was with other kids in the kindergarten room, being supervised by another group member, which they took turns doing.

If some of the mothers had to pay for childcare, they would not have been able to attend the meetings. So, it was another of the many ways that they helped each other out, and all the children knew was that their moms were meeting to talk about "grown-up" stuff.

Of course, you could only shelter children from so much, Bridget knew. They had eyes and ears and took in far more than adults gave them credit for.

You only had to look into Delilah Blume's eyes to understand that.

As Bridget got busy making coffee and arranging cookies and other baking on plates, making sure that Michael's cookies were given center stage, she silently rehearsed what she was going to say to the group.

More women began to arrive, pitching in and greeting one another. Bridget's heart swelled with true affection for them all.

They came from all classes, professions and cultures; some were from Green Valley, while others drove in from small towns nearby. They had little in common other than being victims of abuse, but that was enough. Week by week they helped each other through the painful process of accepting and believing that what happened to them wasn't their fault.

There was an atmosphere of absolute trust in the room and Bridget took it in, sustaining herself, and was ready to speak when the woman leading the group that week asked if anyone wanted to share.

Bridget knew that she would receive their best advice only if she was fully honest, so she didn't allow herself to skim over any of the complex emotions that Sawyer Blume and his daughter raised in her, but did her best to describe Sawyer in as objective a way as possible, despite the fact that even saying his name out loud caused her insides to fizz like a carbonated drink.

"So what do you think?" she concluded. "Should I let him help me or not?"

"What would be your reasons for *not* letting him help you?" a woman named Erna asked. Erna was from a small town nearby. She had been married to a man who found all women enticing except the one he was married to.

Erna was using a tried-and-true group technique: questions always helped the person with the issue think things through and maybe discover that the answer was already there.

"I don't want to depend on anyone," Bridget said. "Especially a man," she added bluntly.

"Why is that?"

"Because… Well, because I don't want to be weak."

"Do you think that needing help makes you weak?" Felicia, one of their most elderly members, asked in a gently puzzled voice. "It seems to me that being able to accept help when we need it is a sign of strength, not weakness. Besides, if you reject help because of your history with Wes, you're still letting him control you in some way."

"Here's what I think," Mavis said in her straightforward way. "I think you're less afraid of accepting help than you are of facing the fact that you might actually care for Sawyer."

Much as she might want to, Bridget knew there was no sense in denying it. The healing and revelations that occurred in the group never happened when things were suppressed.

"I do care," she said softly, looking down at her folded hands. "About him and about his little girl, but I don't think I need to explain why that's hard for me."

The others were silent for a moment; most nodded in understanding.

Then Felicia spoke again. "I think that choosing to love again is about the bravest decision any of us can make."

He should just go home. With two unanswered and two un-listened-to voice mails on his phone, Sawyer knew he really just needed to go home. Especially since the audit at the vet clinic had been done for days and Bridget seemed to have gone back behind her defensive barrier again and was waffling on letting him get involved in her business plans in any way.

Yes, no doubt, he should be packing up right this very minute. Instead, he was at the church, toying on the piano and engaged in conversation with Harold Price, while Delilah was contentedly back at the house with Mildred, learning how to make rhubarb pie.

He was trying to be casual about it—trying to gauge what the chances were that he and Bridget would actually work together on something and he'd have a reason to stay. But he needed to phrase things so that Harold wouldn't zero in like a bird after a worm on other aspects of their relationship.

Okay, so he knew he couldn't stay just for her—it wouldn't be fair to any of them—but he was having a very hard time lately making decisions without her pretty and stubborn face provoking his thoughts.

"So, what do you think Bridget will end up doing now that Dr. Burgess is retiring?" Sawyer asked, tapping one finger lightly and repeatedly on middle C on the piano keyboard.

Dr. Burgess had chosen to share her decision during announcements at the church service on the previous Sunday. So, now many people in town were aware of the situation.

Harold's eyes twinkled shrewdly. "Well, I don't imagine it's anything you need concern yourself with," he said, not unkindly. "Unless there's something you've been keeping to yourself."

Sawyer fought the urge to squirm like someone his daughter's age under Harold's grin and probing eyes. There really was something about the Price siblings that made him want to open up. But Doc B hadn't said anything about the offer on the clinic during her announcement, or about her agreement to give Bridget until September to come up with her own offer, so he didn't know how much he could say.

"I don't just do audits," he said after a minute. He took his hand off the piano, interlinked his fingers and flexed them. "I'm really more of an investor. That's our family business—we invest in properties, buy them out, try to turn a profit."

The latter words tasted sour in his mouth as he spoke them.

"And you're telling me this because…?"

"Because I'm curious, from a business perspective." Even as he said the words, Sawyer knew they rang false and Harold's expression confirmed it.

"I mean," he pressed on regardless, "something has to happen to the property if Dr. Burgess is retiring."

"So, you're just interested in what might happen to the property?" Harold asked. But before Sawyer could answer he said, "But you started this conversation by wondering what Bridget was going to do."

Sawyer shrugged and grinned ruefully. There was no sense in denying it.

"I guess I did."

"It seems to me," Harold said, taking a hanky from his pocket and diligently polishing a spot on the trombone that sat near him, "that, with you being an investor and all, that you'd just be able to look at whether buying the property was a good business decision or not, unless there's a reason why you can't do that."

Again, Sawyer didn't know what he could say without betraying Bridget's trust. It was strange how quickly the urge to protect her had overcome him, even among people who knew her better than he did and wanted what was best for her. Yet, something in him stirred to be her champion, to do what he could to make sure her life turned out the way she wanted.

If she would let him.

Or maybe he just wanted to prove to himself that it wasn't always going to be too late to be there for someone.

"It's more complicated than that," he finally said.

Harold nodded. "It usually is." He looked up from his polishing. "Is Green Valley a place you could see yourself living?"

Sawyer chucked. "You know how to ask the tough questions, Harold, I'll give you that."

"Because," Harold said, not joining in the humor, "if you think it's going to fix whatever you're running from, you're wrong. I know it seems pretty idyllic at first, a small town with unique business opportunities where people know each other. But being here isn't going to fix anything. That comes from here." He pointed a finger at his own heart. "And with the good Lord's help."

"What makes you think I'm running from something?" Sawyer asked, unable to quite meet the other man's eyes. But he felt Harold's steady gaze for a moment before the older man said, "Because we're all running from something, even if it's ourselves."

Sawyer briefly wondered what relief he would experience by telling someone exactly what happened the day that Tina died. But he suddenly thought that if he was ever going to share that with anyone here it would be with Bridget.

Needing to escape the conversation, he turned his full attention to the piano and began to play a Strauss waltz.

"Well," Harold said, "if you need a reason to stay besides that pretty young woman who you refuse to admit has anything to do with it, there's a variety of ways the town could use a good piano player."

"I used to love music," Sawyer said. "I still do, of course." He gave the piano keys an affectionate pat. "I used to dream of a career in music, or at least in teaching others to enjoy it."

"And what happened to that dream?" Harold asked.

"It just wasn't practical." There he went, falling back on that convenient but tired excuse.

"Son," Harold said with kindness, "isn't it about time that you stopped thinking about what's practical and started thinking about what you really want? I don't know where you're at with the Lord, and that's none of my business. But I can tell you that, from my experience, He wants to meet us in our true heart's desires, not where we think we're supposed to be."

"But what if I want the wrong thing?" Sawyer asked.

"He'll let you know."

Sawyer decided that it was high time for him to get on with his day…whatever that would entail.

As he walked back to Mildred's house, he pondered Harold's comments. If he stayed in Green Valley, did he really want to open another investment firm, or was God giving him a chance to follow some heart desires that had been long suppressed?

But then, as if to crush any thought of that, his phone rang and a quick glance told him it was his brother calling. Much as he wanted to ignore it, Sawyer knew he couldn't keep doing that.

"Marc," he said into the phone.

"How's life in Mayberry?" Marc quipped. Then in a more serious tone, he added, "Look, Sawyer, I don't know what—or who—you're wasting time with there but we need you home."

"Dad told me not to bother coming home," Sawyer reminded him. "At least, not to expect to be part of the business, which pretty much means to Dad that I'm not part of the family either."

"He doesn't mean that," Marc said. "Not really."

"Well, I haven't heard otherwise from him."

"Mom wants you to come home. She *needs* you to come home. She's been trying to talk Dad into going for some medical tests but you know how he is."

Guilt ricocheted through Sawyer, even as he told himself that he wouldn't put it past his family to pull out all the stops to keep controlling his life.

"Is Dad still sick?" he asked. "He told me it was nothing." Not that he'd talked to his father in several days.

"Yeah," Marc said. "He's losing weight, doesn't have much appetite."

"I'll call them tonight," Sawyer promised, unwilling to commit to anything else, and even though he still believed he'd be the last person to have any influence on his father right now.

God, he asked with a sinking feeling, *is the past going to keep pulling me back in?*

Because it seemed that no matter how hard he tried, he was never going to be allowed to move on with his life. He put away his phone and walked into Mildred's.

The last person Sawyer expected to see sitting at Mildred's kitchen table was Bridget. But something about the way her hand curved around a glass of milk, a piece of rhubarb pie on a plate in front of her and the questioning and slightly apologetic look she gave him chased his previous dark thoughts away.

Then Delilah bounded toward him, tugging his hand and pointing at a piece of pie meant for him.

"Did you make this?" he asked. "Wow, great job!"

She beamed.

Mildred turned from the sink, revealing a rather floury face. "She was a wonderful helper. She learns very quickly, this little girl."

She briskly dried her hands on a towel. Delilah went to her and pressed into her side and Mildred gave her a one-armed hug.

Sawyer watched, thoughtful. There were getting to be more reasons why it would be hard to leave Green Valley and go home again. Especially, when the word *home* didn't fit the spiritually empty place he had left.

Bridget cleared her throat softly.

"Oh, that's right," Mildred said, releasing Delilah and giving her shoulders a final little squeeze. "Bridget has been waiting to talk to you."

"You're not working today?" Sawyer checked the time.

"I said I needed some time on a personal matter." Bridget lifted her chin. "Besides, we weren't busy."

Sawyer heard the note of worry in her voice as she said the latter. There was no doubt that with Dr. Burgess leaving, the future of the clinic was unclear, and if something didn't change in a hurry they could be opening the door to a big chain sports store.

"Would you like to walk?" Sawyer asked. "Where's Sophie, by the way?"

"She's at home. She'll be fine for a bit."

"Maybe Delilah and I can stop by later to see her. We could all go for a walk."

Bridget's sharp glance darted to him and he wondered, *Why do I say things like that?*

But then she said, "Sure."

Silence and something else hung between them for a moment.

"So," Sawyer said, "you needed some personal time?"

"Yes, I need to talk to you about something."

Delilah looked up from her pie, suddenly still and listening.

"Delilah," Mildred said, "I would really appreciate your help with sprinkling some sugar and cinnamon on the pie crusts. Sawyer— Bridget, the living room is free if you decided you'd rather walk later."

"We might as well just sit there for a minute," Bridget said. "This won't take long."

Lord, Sawyer prayed, *whatever she's about to tell me, please let me deal with it.* Because he now knew beyond doubt that he would be very disappointed if Bridget Connelly wouldn't let him be part of her life in some way, even if it couldn't be on a personal level.

They sat in the welcoming and comforting surroundings of Mildred's living room.

Bridget took a deep breath and folded her hands.

Here comes the part where I might as well face going home, Sawyer thought.

"I've decided that I want you on board with the project," Bridget said.

Relief and gratitude washed through him. He didn't know what his role would be or how long it would mean he would be part of Bridget's life. He just knew that God wasn't finished yet with whatever was between them.

And for now that was more—much more— than he expected.

Chapter Fourteen

Sawyer looked so happy and relieved that it caused a flutter in Bridget's stomach and her carefully crafted speech momentarily took flight.

"Whatever you want, I'm here," Sawyer said, impulsively reaching out and squeezing her hands. "Whatever you need me for, just ask."

She looked down at their hands entwined together and had the distinct impression that she was rescuing him from something as much as he was rescuing her.

No, I don't need to be rescued.

The flurry of conflicting thoughts brought her back to what she had originally intended to say.

As if suddenly aware himself, Sawyer let go of her hands and sat up straighter.

"I mean whatever the business needs," he said briskly. "I'm sure I can help you out with that."

"Right, right," Bridget said, emulating his brisk tone. She had wondered if he was going to ask her how she had come to the decision and had prepared a bit of an answer, but it didn't appear as if they were going to have that conversation. She smiled with relief at not having to offer extensive explanations for her change of heart.

"So, how can I help?" Sawyer asked.

"Well, the first thing is that I'd like it in writing that if you invest financially that I pay you back with interest."

She saw Sawyer's hesitation but then he nodded.

"And I want all of my ideas to be given equal weight," she continued. "If I get any inkling at all that you're not taking me seriously, this ends immediately."

Sawyer blinked in genuine surprise. "Equal weight?" he said. "Your ideas have *all* the weight. Bridget, this is all you. I'm just the grunt in the background who might be able to steer you in some of the right directions."

Bridget swallowed as her emotions threatened to overtake her in an unexpected and decidedly un-businesslike manner. She was making progress, but it was still hard to believe at times that she had something worthwhile to offer.

Her true goal was not to rely on someone

else to tell her that, but still Sawyer's words impacted her deeply.

After the initial barriers were brought down, they delved into an enthusiastic discussion, talking first about some preliminary promotional plans to draw attention to the project. They would put flyers up in the clinic and distribute pamphlets—they would ask Seth if they could do the same at his café—to attract people to a rudimentary presentation.

They also began roughing out a budget and a calendar of when she'd have to accomplish certain goals. It was a lot of work, and he continually reminded her that often business plans seemed daunting until you broke them down into individual steps. The first step would be to explain how people needing companionship and pets needing a home could be brought together, and also how music might be able to help bridge those initial gaps of trust.

"And maybe some long-existing pet-owner relationships could benefit by looking at some different ways of doing things," Bridget added.

"Yes, I'm sure I could put together a lively food jingle for Mr. Snow," Sawyer said with a droll look.

Bridget laughed. "Maybe not such a good idea."

"Maybe not but I think this is." Sawyer

pointed at himself, then at her. "I think that we're a good idea."

Bridget knew that he meant as a business team but pleasant warmth suffused her and her heart whispered that she'd made a good choice to trust someone again.

Thank you, Lord.

She glanced at the time on her phone. "I should be getting back," she said. "But I'll get hold of Seth and we can start getting the word out about needing pets to test the music on.

"We can make a day of it on Saturday," Sawyer agreed as he escorted her to the door.

Despite the sunshine, the air had a mid-August bite to it that temporarily sobered Bridget's mood. She had almost waited too long to let her guard down and allow Sawyer to help her. Doubt nagged at her, asking how much they could really accomplish before Sawyer had to get Delilah back for school. They were going back, weren't they? He hadn't said otherwise.

But, no, she wasn't going to succumb to doubts again. She was going to step forward in faith and see where the journey took her.

Another week passed quickly. Seth was accommodating and it was easy to spread the word in the café and even to get other volunteers to help post and deliver flyers. Sawyer showed Bridget how to make best use of the various social media sites to target residents in the region. She also continued to work with Sophie and found a calm pleasure in how well the dog responded to her instruction.

On Saturday they were joined by a gratifyingly large group of interested people. They had chosen the town community center as a meeting place because it not only offered a piano and meeting rooms, but also had a large outdoor space where they could watch a demonstration if the first part of the presentation caught their interest.

Bridget tugged at her lower lip. She wasn't sure if she was more nervous about presenting to the group or about how Sophie would behave when Mildred and Delilah brought her by at the allotted time.

"You okay?" Sawyer asked as they joined the group walking toward the meeting room.

"Maybe you could present?" Bridget suggested, glancing up at him. "You must have given a hundred presentations, right? Piece of cake for you."

Sawyer touched her wrist, urging her to stop and face him, while the others continued on.

"No, this is going to be all you," he said. "You've got this, I know you do."

"Are you sure?"

"Absolutely," Sawyer said with emphasis. "Not a single doubt in my mind. Now, Sophie," he added with a teasing note that brought levity to the moment, "I'm not so sure of."

"I'm just teasing," he reassured Bridget, as slight panic wobbled her laughter. "She'll be fine. You'll be fine. You'll be more than fine, you'll be wonderful."

Bridget searched his face, wondering exactly when it had started to be like a familiar book she had read many times for comfort.

"Okay," she said.

Half an hour later it was over and Bridget basked in the exhausted but elated glow of successfully getting through a challenge.

A few people had decided that what was being offered wasn't for them or were skeptical about its possibilities. But a respectable number chose to stay around and watch the demonstration.

As promised, Mildred and Delilah were waiting outside with Sophie. Pink ribbons adorned the little girl's pigtails, but her shorts were blue denim and her top was blue and white striped.

Her face lit up when she saw them, while Sophie yipped and wagged her greeting.

"Okay, Soph," Bridget said, scratching the happy dog behind both ears. "It's showtime. Delilah, you know what to do."

Delilah's grin spread across her face like a

beacon of all that was fun and surprising in the world. It wasn't often that a little girl was encouraged to be rowdy. Bridget only hoped that the novelty of it all would keep at bay any nerves about people watching.

She didn't need to worry. Delilah jumped and frolicked, ran in circles and clapped her hands, encouraging Sophie to romp and frolic with her.

When Sophie was good and wound up, Bridget took out her phone and held it high, while Sawyer gestured to her getting everyone's attention.

Holding her breath and saying a hurried silent prayer, Bridget pushed Play and "The Blue Danube" waltz filled the air with its glorious strains.

For about fifteen heart-stopping seconds she wondered if it was going to work. They had been working diligently with Sophie, and with thorough and repetitive practice were getting her to associate the song with soft, soothing voices, gentle pats and reassurance that she was loved and in a safe place. But Sophie was in a very excited state and she was in an unfamiliar atmosphere. Then she stopped romping and her head tilted as the music reached her. She let out a few soft barks, turned in a circle and lay down with a sigh. Delilah immediately dropped to her knees beside her and, as she had been taught, patted her friend gently, murmuring that she was a good, good dog.

The watching crowd erupted in a small burst of applause.

"Well, I'll be," Dudley, the pharmacist, said. "I've never seen anything like it."

There was a flurry of questions and answers. For the first few, Bridget glanced at Sawyer for his input but his encouraging nod gave her the confidence to field the questions.

"Does it only work with that song?" someone asked.

"No, any song you choose could work," Bridget explained. "The key is the consistency and getting your pet to associate the song with feeling soothed and comforted."

"I don't have one of those new phones," an elderly woman fretted. "And I don't plan to get one. Technology gives me a headache. I do have a piano," she added thoughtfully. "But I haven't touched it since my kids grew up and stopped taking piano lessons."

"Sawyer plays the piano," Bridget said. "Sawyer, would you be willing to give Mrs. Jacobs a refresher?"

Sawyer had been brushing up on his music skills using the piano at the church and told Bridget that picking out long-forgotten but still-familiar tunes was a kind of healing in itself.

"I feel like I've come home," he had said.

Bridget hoped now that she wasn't overstepping her boundaries but things had gone so well today that it reminded her that the girl who made plans and believed in their good results still lived somewhere within the nervous creature she had become.

Or maybe she was just thinking about what it would be like if Green Valley really did become Sawyer's home and she wanted to find as many reasons as possible for him to stay as she could.

"I'm a bit rusty myself," Sawyer said, in a careful but calm way. "But, sure, I can give it a try."

"This isn't just for pets with severe behavioral problems," Bridget reminded the group as things were wrapping up. "This is something that can be used to comfort both you and your pet. And, if you've been thinking about companionship and giving a home to an animal that needs one, this could be a way to ease through those first days of adjustment."

When all was said and done, four people signed up for the training. It wasn't a lot but it was enough to give Bridget something to move forward with.

"Sawyer, Bridget," Mildred said as she came up beside them, "that went well, didn't it? I'm sure the two of you would like some time to debrief, as they say. Sophie is welcome in my backyard. Maybe we'll have a picnic. It's hard to believe now but it won't be long until it's too chilly to do that until next summer."

Bridget couldn't help wondering if Sawyer heard the same thing in Mildred's voice whenever she uttered the words "you two"—like she was about to start planning a wedding.

It was somehow not an unpleasant thought.

But her words also sent a pang of regret through Bridget. Even before Wes, something about the change in the air when summer slipped into fall always filled her with a kind of nostalgia for missed opportunities.

However, she reminded herself that now was the time to move forward—*finally, thank you, Lord*—and today was just the beginning.

So, before she changed her mind, she reached out in a demonstration of trust and asked Sawyer, "Would you like to come to my place for a glass of lemonade?"

Sawyer knew it was an act of trust for Bridget to extend that invitation.

It was getting harder to think about leaving her, even harder than the thought of going home at all. He wasn't sure what home meant to him anymore.

A few nights ago, he had yielded to the guilt

over missed phone calls. When he spoke to his father, though, Hank Blume sounded more tired than usual. Nonetheless, his attitude had not changed.

"What do you want?" he had snapped. "You've made your disinterest in this family clear, so I'm not sure why you're calling now."

"Mom and Marc say you've been ill." Sawyer prayed silently that he wouldn't give in to the urge to snap back or to immaturely end the phone call. "I thought I should get in touch."

"Oh, did you? Well, don't do me any favors." It was his father who ended the call.

A few minutes later his mother had called back, speaking in a hushed voice. "Your father has never known how to ask for help," she tried to explain. "He lashes out when he's hurt. He doesn't mean any of it."

But her words didn't help bridge the ever-widening gap. It only made Sawyer more frustrated over the way his mother always tried to smooth things over, leaving his father with no responsibility for the way he could alienate his sons.

Marc was closer to their father than he would ever be, but Sawyer knew he would never be willing to live in Hank's back pocket to attain that closeness.

Those days were behind him. He just wished he knew what the days ahead would hold.

"Are you okay?" Bridget asked. She hesitated with the key in her front door.

"Yes." Sawyer gave his head a mental shake. "Yes, I'm good."

"Come in," Bridget said and he stepped through the foyer into the open space of the living room. She made a hesitant sweeping gesture and said, "So, this is it—my humble abode."

The movement caused her hair to stir gently and the subtle scent of sweet apples tantalized Sawyer.

Sawyer observed Bridget's home with keen interest. He immediately got a strong sense of her in the open floor plan, the clean lines and the fresh, bright colors. But it wasn't perfectly immaculate and, just as he loved the way there were always rebellious hairs that escaped her ponytail, he found the lived-in touches appealing. There was a magazine open on the coffee table and a Bible and a bookmarked devotional beside it. Knowing her struggles in faith were similar to his, he wondered how long they'd been there and how often—if ever—she looked at them these days.

A mug featuring the cartoonish faces of a dog and a cat stood on a side table placed at the end of a tan couch, and a basket of carefully folded but not yet put away laundry was in the entrance to the hallway.

Bridget's own eyes darted around the room, taking all of it in.

"Sorry, it's kind of a mess." She hurried the mug into the kitchen and returned to lift the basket of laundry.

"Don't worry," Sawyer said. "I like it. It feels like home."

There was that word again. It hung between them. Bridget stood glued in place, the basket hoisted.

"I'll be right back," she said, breaking up the unintended import of the words. She flew down the hallway.

Sawyer picked up the devotional and studied it thoughtfully. The subject of the book was finding God in dark places and his heart ached for the reason that Bridget would need it. She returned to the room and hesitated at seeing it in his hands.

He carefully put it back on the table and his mind raced with hundreds of questions, the main one being if the devotional was helping her in any way.

He wondered if there was anything he could read or study that would help him deal with how he had lost his wife and Delilah, her mother.

And with the constant sense of failure that loomed over him.

But Bridget didn't open the conversation and

instead passed by him into the kitchen. "I said lemonade but I have iced tea too if you like that better."

"Lemonade is great," Sawyer said, following her into the kitchen. "What can I do to help?"

"Nothing, have a seat." Bridget gestured to one of the tall, light-colored wooden stools that lined the kitchen counter. The kitchen too was a wide-open, sunny space, painted white with accents of calming shades of blue. Again, Sawyer looked for glimpses that would tell him more about the woman who busily emptied an ice cube tray into a glass pitcher and ran water into it.

She opened the refrigerator door and found lemons and then rummaged in one of the kitchen drawers for a knife and began to rapidly slice lemons.

"Ow!" Bridget suddenly blurted in shock, releasing the knife and letting it tumble onto the counter. Sawyer was immediately on his feet, as he saw her fingertips split open with a thin thread of blood.

"Are you okay?" He was by her side in an instant, as she stared at her fingers like she'd never seen them before. It was only when he grasped her hand to study the damage that she snapped out of it and said, shaking her head. "I'm fine, just clumsy. I wasn't paying attention to what I was doing."

Sawyer held the injured fingers up, looking closely at them. "It doesn't look deep, so that's a good thing," he said. "You won't need stitches. Wait just a minute, don't move."

He let her hand go and pulled a hanky out of his back pocket, then he retrieved her hand and dabbed at her fingers.

It was hard to resist the urge to lift her hand to his mouth and to kiss the injured fingers one by one.

"Do you have bandages?" he asked instead.

"Yes, I'll go fix myself up." Bridget pulled her hand away and gave him back the hanky. She wouldn't quite meet his eyes and Sawyer had the sensation that she knew his thoughts.

While she was gone, he wiped up the counter and carefully sliced the rest of the lemon, which was untainted by her accident.

Bridget returned with her fingers bandaged, hiding from the unexpected intimacy of the moment behind the teasing smile on her face.

"Thank you for letting me use your hanky," she said. "I don't think I've seen one of those since my grandpa had one."

"Actually...it was a present from Tina," Sawyer said. "I'm not exactly sure why I still carry it. I guess I just..."

"You carry it because it was a present from her," Bridget said, quickly sobering. "I'm sorry

I didn't know. Thank you for letting me use it. I'll—I'll pay to get it cleaned."

Sawyer shook his head, not wanting Bridget to feel badly because his late wife had come into the conversation. He had loved Tina and he missed her. But when he was with Bridget he realized that life could go on and he knew that he wanted it to.

"It was really more of a joke present than anything," he hurried to explain. "Believe me, Tina thought hankies were as old-fashioned as you do. But she always liked to tease me about being so businesslike and not letting loose. She said it made me old before my time and that I should carry a hanky like an elderly man did and then she gave me one."

"And you still carry it." Bridget nodded as if she would expect nothing less.

"I don't know why do." His heart tugged in two different directions, wanting to be loyal to Tina's memory but wanting to reassure the woman right in front of him, here and now, that he didn't intend her to compete with those memories.

Bridget had given him the gift of her trust by sharing her secret and now by inviting him into her home. And, now he felt the Lord urging him to return that gift by trusting her with the story of the night that Tina had died.

"We were going to have a family movie night," he began without preamble, hoping—praying—that Bridget would understand the words that wanted now to rush out of him, because he didn't think he could stop them if he tried.

"I went out to get snacks. I'm sure I wasn't even gone for twenty minutes. When I got home, I knew as soon as I opened the door that something was wrong. Or, maybe I just think now that I knew." He shook his head. Bridget's eyes were on him like a soothing caress.

"The house was quiet, too quiet."

He swallowed.

"I found them in the kitchen. Tina was—dead—on the floor. Delilah was sitting beside her. That's when she started whispering. She told me later that they'd gotten into a bit of an argument, probably about something silly, I don't know about what. She said, 'I yelled at Mommy and she fell over.'"

"And she hasn't spoken in a full voice since," Bridget said, her own voice raw with dreadful understanding.

Sawyer nodded. "It was a blood clot, I found out later. It burst in her brain. We had no warning. But I can't help thinking that I should have noticed something—*anything*—and if I hadn't been working so much all the time, maybe I would have."

"Sawyer, I'm so, so sorry," Bridget said, moving to stand more closely beside him. "But it wasn't your fault. You couldn't have known. There's nothing you could have done."

"I've been carrying it with me for a long time," Sawyer said, and a weariness that was strangely restful crept through him. "I'm glad I told you. I don't know if I can accept what you've said, at least not yet. But I am glad."

After a moment, Bridget silently offered him back his hanky.

But he pressed it back into her hand. "You keep this," he said, his voice almost a whisper. "I don't... I don't need it anymore." He hoped his eyes conveyed all that he meant by that. He wasn't just letting go of a square of white material. He was trying to show her that her words—that she—meant something to him, even if he wasn't able to fully forgive himself.

His eyes must have told her something, for suddenly she was in his arms and she was kissing him—*she was kissing him!*—and tears sprang to his eyes, startling him, but he let them run down his cheeks as he kissed her back and all the reasons he could think of for why it couldn't work for them disappeared into this one, heart-changing moment.

Bridget stepped back but kept her palms on the side of her face. "I'm so sorry," she said softly. "I didn't mean to make you cry. We don't have to talk about your wife anymore. It must be so painful to be reminded."

"No," Sawyer said. He pressed his hands over hers, then gently removed them from his face. "No, these aren't sad tears. They're…" He shook his head with a small smile. "Well, to be honest, I don't know exactly what these are. I think I just feel more—free—than I've felt for a long time. It's like for the first time in months I can believe that Delilah and I are going to get through this."

Nothing meant more to Sawyer in that moment than the shining eyes of the woman who told him, while the taste of her strawberry lip gloss lingered, that she believed the same thing.

Chapter Fifteen

"You will," Bridget encouraged. "I know you will." She hugged him briefly again.

"Let's go outside," she urged. "I can finish making the lemonade and we can sit and chat more."

Sawyer lifted her hand and kissed her bandaged fingertips. "I think I'd better finish up in the kitchen," he teased. "I'll see you out there."

The back porch was one of Bridget's favorite parts of the house. It was a spacious area with wicker furniture heaped with cushions, assorted round tables to hold drinks and snacks, and baskets filled with magazines. Often, however, Bridget liked to just sit and contemplate, engaging God in prayer and seeking His will for her life, although she hadn't done much of that lately.

Yet, it seemed now that the Lord was giving

her every signal that she could be happy again, that she was *allowed* to be happy again.

"You look lost in thought," Sawyer commented, easing through the open patio door with a glass of lemonade in each hand. He set them down on a table between the two chairs and sat, taking in the surroundings. "You have a lovely home," he said. "It reminds me of you. It's beautiful but it's approachable too. It's got a good heart," he chuckled, "if you can say that about a house."

Bridget took in his compliment, picked up her lemonade and sipped thoughtfully. It was lovely to hear a man say flattering things to her again, especially since she was sure that Sawyer Blume was not the kind of man to fill a woman's head with empty compliments. But, despite the kiss that she had instigated, she had to keep a grip on herself. She had come a long way from the woman who lived for those compliments.

"What are you thinking about?" Sawyer asked, sounding slightly anxious. "I hope I didn't cross a boundary, because that's the last thing I would want to do."

"I kissed you," Bridget reminded him.

"Yes, you did. Is that what's bothering you?"

She shifted in her chair. "I never said that anything was bothering me."

"No, but something has changed since you came outside," Sawyer said. "Besides, you don't have to say anything. Your eyes are not only the most remarkable shade of blue—they also spell your moods out loud and clear."

"Okay, I guess that's what's bothering me," Bridget said, moving to the edge of her chair while anxiety began to creep through her.

Sawyer tilted his head with a puzzled look. "You don't want me to ask you if there's something wrong?"

"I don't want you to compliment me," Bridget said. "I don't want either of us to lose sight of what we're doing here."

Sawyer set his drink on a table and studied his hands for a moment, reaching to push up his glasses when they began to slide down his nose.

"But that's just it," he said, raising his gaze to hers. "What exactly *are* we doing here because I don't think I know anymore, do you?"

Bridget opened her mouth to answer, then shrugged helplessly. "I know what I'm supposed to be doing. I didn't expect my feelings to get so—complicated."

"So you're struggling with that too?" Sawyer acknowledged with a sad smile.

"And why do you think that is?" Bridget asked with her churning nerves uncertain about whether or not she really wanted to hear the answer.

"You're part of it," Sawyer said bluntly. "I'm not trying to flatter you and I hope you know I don't believe in empty praise. But you're so determined to overcome your personal setbacks and be a better and stronger person, and you care so much for your community, I guess it's made me think about what I want for the future for Delilah and me, what I want going forward."

Suddenly restless, Bridget stood up and paced a little. *Please Lord, calm me. Help me to stay focused on my goal. I'm so confused. I don't know what's best.*

Bridget quelled her emotions behind her folded arms. "But regardless of what you decide," she said, keeping her voice tuneless because she didn't trust it, "you live somewhere else and you have a life to get back to."

She fought against the regret that wanted to yank her back down into the darkness she had worked so hard to come out of. There was no need for it. Life was never going to be exactly the way she wanted it to be, but it never would be for anyone, not when they were on this side of Heaven. But she had much to be grateful for and she could sincerely thank God for that.

"But I do appreciate the help you're willing

to give me as long as you do stay," she quickly amended. She took a sip of her lemonade. "Things did go well today, didn't they?" She smiled.

Before Wes, it really had been her nature to focus on the positive and to believe that everything was going to work out for the best. She was making a tentative journey back to being that person and she didn't want to retrace her steps, regardless of what happened.

"They did," Sawyer agreed. "And it was all you, Bridget. You have a way with people and everyone can see the passion you have for what you want to do."

"Delilah and Sophie did a great job too."

"Do you think they were maybe a little too into it?" Sawyer asked jokingly.

"Maybe just a smidge."

They laughed together and Bridget thought about what a gift it was to share easy laughter with someone: a gift she thought she would never get back.

Thank you, Lord. I do believe You are with me and I realize now that You've been with me in all of this. Please forgive me for doubting You.

Bridget noticed that Sawyer had gone quiet. He lifted his glass to eye level and slowly turned it in his hand, thoughtfully watching the ice rotate.

"If something is wrong with the lemonade, remember it was you who made it," she quipped.

Sawyer smiled and shook his head. He put the glass down and turned to her. "What if I stayed?"

It was the hottest part of the day, the time when you could forget that fall was on its way and the air suddenly seemed to shimmer briefly, sunlight bouncing like diamonds off of their glasses of lemonade.

"Stayed?" Bridget repeated like she'd never heard the word before.

"Yes, Delilah and I. What if we stayed in Green Valley?"

A mosaic of thoughts clamored for attention in Bridget's head as she tried to decipher what her true reaction was to hearing his unexpected suggestion.

"You don't approve?" Sawyer said into her silence, trying for but not quite pulling off a light, bantering tone.

His question helped her thoughts crystallize. "Why would you stay?" she asked. She probably sounded more blunt than she'd intended but, whatever her reasons for wishing him to stay, it was important that he had his own ones, separate from her desires.

Much as she had grown to care for Sawyer and Delilah, and much as her heart panged with hurt over how he had lost his wife, she didn't want him to imagine that she was in any kind of place to rescue him from his pain.

Sawyer drummed his fingers on the table beside him, a gesture Bridget had learned meant he was thinking and, perhaps, troubled.

"When you asked me if I could give Mrs.... Jacobs..."

Bridget nodded, confirming he had remembered the name correctly.

"When you asked me if I could give Mrs. Jacobs a refresher on the piano," Sawyer continued, "it clarified some things for me. Some things I've been trying to sort out since I got here."

"I didn't mean to put you on the spot with that," Bridget said. "It just jumped into my head in the moment."

"No, no, it's fine, it really is." Sawyer sat forward and swiveled in his chair to face her directly, letting her see the sincerity in his face.

"For the longest time," he said slowly, as if he was searching for words, "I thought I had to choose between two worlds. I thought I could either pursue the things I was passionate about when I was younger, like music, or I could do the responsible thing like join the family business and work hard to make money and make a good life for my family.

"But what good was it all?" he continued, clenching his hands on his knees. "What I mean is that all the money in the world couldn't change what happened to Tina and, like I've said, if I'd been working less maybe I would have been paying more attention."

Bridget shook her head, but didn't interrupt. She reached out and stroked his wrist with her fingers.

"It was that way when I worked with my father," Sawyer said. His gaze fell on her hand and something pulsed between them before he continued to speak. "I mean it was an all-or-nothing scenario. I was either working or carving out time with Tina and Delilah, out of whatever left-over time there was to carve from, that is. There was no time to even remember what I used to care about." He paused and lightly drummed his fingers on the side of his glass as he sought the right words.

"I feel like here there is the possibility that I could do both. I don't expect to make a living at my music, but there's no reason why I couldn't work in investments and officially join the music group at church or help people like Mrs. Jacobs learn how to play the piano. Really, anything is possible."

Sawyer's face was lit with such hopeful joy that Bridget almost hated to ask her next question but she had to know. She had to be sure that she was *not* the reason he wanted to stay in Green Valley. Because, no matter how attracted she was to him, no matter how much she cared about him and Delilah, she still had too much to do to get her own life back on track.

So she asked, "Couldn't you do that anywhere? I mean, now that you realize it's possible, does it have to be here?"

"Trying to get rid of me?" Sawyer joked, but behind his glasses his eyes scrutinized her. He grinned then, gentling the comment.

He shook his head. "No, I get what you're saying, I do. But I do like it here and I see a lot of potential here. I like the idea of being able to be involved with people and their dreams on a more personal level. And Delilah…" He stopped and shook his head. He looked down at his hands, his fingers slowed and stilled and he gazed back up into Bridget's face.

She almost reeled back at the unvarnished vulnerability that was there.

"I wish you could have seen what Delilah was like before we came here," Sawyer said. "Actually, maybe I don't. It was like living with a small, black cloud that stayed after a devastating storm. But if you'd seen that you would understand what being in Green Valley has done for her so far. She's *trusting* people again. Who knows, maybe she'll even start talking again. For the first time in a long time, I believe it's possible for her, and there wasn't a single therapist we saw that could help me believe that."

He reached out to Bridget, offering her his open hands. Without hesitation, she slid her hands into his.

"She trusts you," Sawyer said, giving her hands a gentle squeeze. "I trust you and hope I can always give you reason to feel the same way about me. Bridget, I know you're still on your own journey but I want you to know that I'm here for you in whatever way you need me to be. I admire your strength and your courage. No matter what happens, I want you to know that you'll always have a friend in me."

Unexpected tears shimmered behind Bridget's eyes. There was nothing more powerful than hope and it seemed that God's timing had ordained that they would share this gift together.

At least for this moment, she decided not to care what it meant or what the future would bring. She wanted to kiss Sawyer again. She leaned toward him, her eyes questioning, his answering yes. She kissed him and that kiss held all of the hope and trust she had to give.

* * *

There was a God. It was a cloudy day the following Wednesday, but Sawyer was in a sunny mood and had never been so sure of his creator's existence.

He had always accepted the existence of God and, up until the moment that his life had irrevocably fallen apart, he'd lived with the self-satisfaction of believing that God must be pleased with him because his life was exactly the way he wanted it to be: a beautiful wife, an adorably feisty little girl and a successful career.

Then Tina died, his beliefs shattered and he experienced the darkest time of his life. It wasn't until he came here to Green Valley and saw the difference that the little town and its people were making to Delilah—the difference they could make in his own life—that he grasped the indescribable experience of finding God on the other side of the darkness and realizing that He had been there the whole time, carrying him through.

Of the many things and people he was thankful for, Bridget Connelly daily took up an increasingly large space in Sawyer's mind and healing heart.

Since Bridget had decided to give him her trust, she had opened up like a sunflower turning its face to its namesake. She was brimming with ideas, and with every moment they spent together, polishing her business plan, Sawyer was treated to ever-widening glimpses of a confident woman who was also experiencing renewed trust in a God who had carried her through.

She also showed her compassion and generosity over his situation by insisting that the money come through in the form of a bank loan and that he focus on his own business and putting down roots in Green Valley.

Of course, there was still so much to think about: now that he was fully committed to helping her attain the clinic space for herself, he still had to find somewhere he could use to open up his own business and, even more importantly, he had to find a house where he and Delilah could live.

Speaking of Delilah, this was the morning he was going to sit down with her and ask her how she would feel about staying. He was fairly confident that he knew the answer, but he looked forward to seeing her reaction.

He had shared the news about his decision with Mildred the night before. She had been enormously pleased, managing to work in a comment about "the two of you spending more time together," even though he hadn't mentioned Bridget's name.

Now, Mildred made sure that Sawyer and Delilah were settled with cheesy scrambled eggs and rye toast, along with their respective coffee and apple juice, before excusing herself to a quilting club meeting at the church.

Sawyer's heart swelled with affection when he looked at his little girl. There was a dollop of grape jelly at the side of her mouth and her hair needed a good brushing, but the contentment on her face overrode all of that.

The untied ribbon that dangled from a tangled clump of her hair was blue and that gave him an extra boost of encouragement.

"Dee-Dee," he began, "you've been happy here, haven't you?"

She nodded and jabbed her fork into her eggs.

"I think you like Mildred a lot, don't you? And… Bridget?"

"And Sophie," Delilah whispered. "And Tyson and Max and Michael."

"That's right. Even though we haven't been here for very long, you've made a lot of friends."

Delilah nodded.

Sawyer took a deep breath. Here came the moment of truth.

"How would you feel about staying?"

The forkful of eggs stopped halfway to her mouth.

"Staying?" she asked, her eyes going wide.

"Yes, if we could find a house here, if you could go to school with Tyson and your other friends, would you want to stay?"

"Would I get to see Sophie every day?"

"That would be up to Bridget," Sawyer said, noting the little extra beat in his pulse when he said her name. "But I'm sure we will see a lot of both of them."

"What about Grandma and Grandpa and Uncle Marc and everybody?" Delilah asked, tugging at her lower lip.

"They can visit and we can visit them anytime you want." Sawyer quelled his uneasiness as the question brought the reminder that he would have to tell his family. But knowing that his father didn't want him home—something he would certainly never share with Delilah—only reinforced his belief that he was making the right choice.

Delilah was still thoughtful, pondering, and he silently prayed that she too would see that it was the right thing. Yes, he was the parent and he could make the decisions but he wouldn't be making this decision if he hadn't seen the strides his daughter had made in the weeks they'd been here.

"I like it here," Delilah whispered. "But Daddy…"

Sawyer watched as his little girl tried to find

words for something no child her age should have to express.

"I don't want anyone else to go away, okay? I want everyone to stay where they are."

The truth was that he couldn't promise her that, not with life's unpredictability. He gathered her into his arms and held her tight. "I'm here, Delilah, I'm here."

For now, it seemed that was enough, because she relaxed into his hug and eventually raised her small face to his.

"Daddy?"

"Yes, Dee-Dee?"

"Can I get my own dog? Can I play music for her? I want to name her Sadie."

Sawyer laughed as the joy of a new start rushed through him. "Maybe," he said. "We'll have to talk more about it. It's one thing to help with Sophie but having your own dog is a big responsibility."

Delilah squeaked.

"I said maybe," Sawyer cautioned, but Delilah had already jumped off his knee and was spinning across the room, opening her arms wide as if to embrace the world.

"I'm almost finished writing my final paper," Bridget told him on the phone later that evening.

"I'd be happy to give it a read through, if you want another set of eyes on it," Sawyer said.

"I may take you up on that."

They had been seeing each other most evenings, mostly with Delilah and Sophie. They would take walks in the park, pop into Seth's for tea and perhaps to share one of his many sweet concoctions. They allowed the well-meaning citizens of Green Valley to speculate hopefully by sitting together in church.

If they didn't see each other, they were developing a comfortable phone habit.

Sawyer was glad that he now knew what Bridget's home looked like. He liked being able to picture her there as he listened to her talk about her day.

His own days were increasingly busy. It was hard to believe that he thought he would be in and out of this little town in just a few days, this little town where he now wanted to plan a new life. Not only was he spending more quality time with his daughter, but there were also home and business real estate options to consider.

He committed himself to being a regular participant in the music ministry at church and spoke to Charlotte Belvedere about getting Delilah enrolled in school for September.

But, although these were all real, necessary

and meaningful parts of his life, he could no longer deny to himself that it was Bridget who was the beacon that shone at the center of it all.

He knew she wasn't ready for a relationship and there was no guarantee she ever would be. He wasn't sure if he would ever be ready again himself to open his heart to that extent.

But their friendship and the trust she placed in it meant everything in the world to him.

"Doc B popped into the clinic," Bridget told him.

"Oh? How are things? What did she have to say?"

"Her days with her mother are challenging." Bridget's voice brimmed with sympathy and Sawyer could picture her twirling a strand of her hair around her finger in a slow and thoughtful way.

"I can only imagine," Sawyer said. His thoughts darted to his own parents. His borderline estrangement from them was the only thing marring his happiness, so he didn't let his thoughts linger there for long.

"Did she say anything about the sale?" he asked instead.

"Just that she managed to postpone her answer with them for another month or so." Bridget's voice went tense with worry. "I just hope I have what I need by then."

"You will," Sawyer reassured her. "Plus, not to sound like a broken record, but I'm here for help if you need me."

"I appreciate that," Bridget said. "I really do, but you've got enough on your plate and you know how much it means to me to prove that I can do this on my own."

That was the thing—Sawyer did know. He felt like he understood Bridget perfectly and he couldn't remember the last time he had felt that way, maybe not even with Tina.

He had loved Tina and he never would have chosen to be apart from her. But, in retrospect, it was very evident to him that they had led quite separate lives. He had already made himself a secret and solemn promise, a promise that was already coming true within his friendship with Bridget.

He promised that if he ever fell in love again and was ready to put his whole heart into a relationship, he would pay attention. He would know what mattered deeply to his love, what her needs were, what she wanted most out of life, and he would support her every step of the way.

Even knowing that nothing would develop beyond friendship, Bridget Connelly was still helping him be the man he wanted to be.

He was just about to ask her more about what Charlotte's best teacher tips were for helping

Delilah get adjusted to a new school when his phone chimed an incoming text.

"Sorry, can you hold on just a minute?" Sawyer asked. "I'm getting a message."

"Sure, go ahead," Bridget encouraged.

Sawyer took the phone away from his ear and looked at the screen. Mild curiosity gelled into immediate panic.

Urgent, his brother Marc's text said. Call home immediately.

Chapter Sixteen

"I—I have to go," Sawyer sputtered into the phone.

"Sawyer, what's wrong?" Bridget asked. "Is it Delilah?"

"No, it's— I don't know for sure. Something is wrong at home. I really just have to go. I'm so sorry."

He only vaguely registered her reassurances that she was there if he needed anything and hoped that his answer to her was polite enough when all he could think about was hanging up.

A deep sense of foreboding stumbled his fingers as he scrolled his recent contacts for his brother's phone number.

Marc answered on the half ring and they barely blurted out greetings before Marc said, "Dad is dying—the doctors say he's only got weeks. He's fighting an aggressive cancer. He didn't want Mom to tell us." His voice turned momentarily granite. "Don't even get me started on that. You've got to come home, bro, *now*."

Like his life flashing before his eyes, a thousand thoughts seemed to run through Sawyer's head at the same time: the fact that his father had made it clear that he wasn't wanted at home anymore; the promises he had made to Bridget; the fact that yet another world that Delilah had known was about to shatter.

But there was only one answer he could give. "I'll be there as soon as I can. We'll leave as soon as we're packed."

Sawyer relayed the news to Mildred, trusting himself only to use terse words.

"Please tell Bridget," he said. "I'll get in touch with her when I can."

Mildred's eyes didn't judge but they were troubled and he knew that he was taking the easy way out, if *easy* was even a word you could use in the situation. He just couldn't bear the thought of saying goodbye, because, of course it would have to be goodbye.

Once he got back—it wasn't home anymore— he would help to care for his father for whatever time he had left, then his mother would have needs, there was the business and how his father's death would impact it. He couldn't dump all of that on Marc.

No, there was no way that God could expect him to deal with all of that and handle saying goodbye to someone he had grown to love.

Grown to love. I love Bridget Connelly.

But she couldn't know that, not now when he couldn't even be there for the things he had promised to be there for, let alone promise her a future.

"Please, Mildred," he added. "I wouldn't ask this of you except…"

"I'll do this for you," Mildred said. "I see what this news has done to you, and Sawyer, I am sending all my prayers to you and your family. But I also pray that you trust that things don't have to end here."

Mildred meant well but she clearly didn't understand his family demands, even at the best of times. He never should have deceived himself—and others along with him: even without a medical emergency, one way or another, he would have been drawn back. He realized now how futile it had been to believe otherwise.

But all he said was "Thank you, Mildred."

Now he had to try to find some way to explain to Delilah why they had to leave and that it was quite certain that they would never be coming back.

All of these other thoughts were assaulted by guilt over his falling-out with his father.

"Do you know where Delilah is?" he asked Mildred.

"She's looking at books in her room," Mildred said. She stepped forward and gave Sawyer a brief, hard hug. She smelled of sugar and lemony furniture polish.

Help me do this, God, Sawyer prayed as he went to Delilah's room. *You're the only one who can.*

This time he wouldn't turn his back on God. This time he planned to cling to Him with everything he had.

Delilah was sprawled on her stomach across the bed, her chin resting in her hands, her elbows resting on an open book.

She looked up, pleased to see him. "Hi, Daddy," she whispered.

"What are you reading?" Sawyer asked in a feeble attempt to stall the inevitable.

Delilah rolled herself into a sitting position and held up the book so he could see the cover. Not surprisingly, it was another story about dogs.

Sawyer sighed and sat down on the edge of her bed.

"Dee-Dee," he said, "I have to talk to you about something. Come sit here close to me."

She snuggled in beside him and he put his arm around her shoulder.

How am I going to tell her this, Lord? How can I possibly find the words?

The answer came that the only possible way was to just do it. It was a cold comfort to remind himself that his daughter, at only seven years old, had already been through worse.

"Dee-Dee... Well, the thing is, Grandpa Hank is very sick, and he needs us at home."

Delilah stiffened beside him.

"Is he going to die?" she whispered.

That was another thing: you could be only seven years old but once you had experienced death, death was always a possibility.

He couldn't lie to her. "It doesn't look good." Then he added, "Yes, sweetheart, the doctors say that Grandpa could die."

"You said no one else would leave." Her voice got louder. She pulled away from him and jumped to her feet, clasping her hands in small fists, and her face reddened as it scrunched into sorrow and anger.

Sawyer clenched a clump of hair in his own fist. Now was not the right time to say that he hadn't exactly made that promise, especially when he had let her believe that he had. Instead he said, "I'm so sorry, I shouldn't have made a promise that's beyond my control to keep."

Delilah chewed her lip and yanked on a piece

of her hair. "How long until we can come back? Will I still be able to go to school with Tyson?"

Sawyer slowly shook his head and it was like dragging a painful weight from one side to the other. "We're going back to stay, Dee-Dee. Grandma will need us. The family needs us."

"No!" Delilah hollered, stomping her foot. "You said we could stay! You said I could go to school here! You said I could maybe get a dog! I don't want to go back home where Mommy died. I don't, I don't, I don't!"

The moment Sawyer had so long waited for had finally arrived—Delilah was back in full voice. But any joy he had anticipated experiencing was drowned out by the sound of utter betrayal in her voice.

The only clear thought he had was that he had made the right decision in asking Mildred to explain things to Bridget. His quota for letting people down was not only full, but spilling out all over the place.

It was the middle of October and Bridget still missed Sawyer Blume and that sweet little girl of his.

She wasn't angry at the way he had left, not exactly, and she grieved silently along with him for what he was going through. But there was no denying that it hurt that he hadn't brought her the news himself. The trust they had built between them meant the world to her and he had thought it was the same for him. Apparently she was wrong, despite what others said to try to appease her. Sawyer had contacted her—but only through brief text messages. Knowing that he was hurting as he dealt with his family crisis did little to ease her pain. She prayed for patience.

Bridget and Charlotte sat bundled in sweaters, sipping pumpkin-spiced tea on Bridget's porch, which she was always determined to use until the snow fell.

"It must have been such a shock to him," Charlotte said. She sat with her feet tucked up under her and blew on her tea. "Did he know his father was sick?"

"I think he might have suspected something," Bridget said. "But from what I gathered about his family, his dad is definitely a workhorse who doesn't believe in stopping for anything. I don't know if anyone realized how bad it was."

"Or were willing to face it," Charlotte added thoughtfully. "You know, Bridge, maybe Sawyer just didn't want to burden you… Maybe he just knew it was going to be too hard for him to say goodbye."

"Oh, I don't know, Char. We were potential business partners. I doubt he was getting that emotionally involved." She shoved aside the memories of the kisses and the confidences they had shared. She wasn't going to go back to hiding behind the wall that had been constructed of self-doubt and fear, but that didn't mean she had to torment herself thinking about things that would never be.

But Charlotte shook her head, her beautiful violet eyes knowing. "I know you don't really believe that, Bridge. Something was happening between you and Sawyer."

"Well, whether or not something was happening, it isn't anymore. He left and he got Mildred to tell me why, and he's barely been in touch, except a few texts." Suddenly restless, Bridget stood up. "More tea?"

Charlotte raised an eyebrow at her. "I haven't even had a sip."

Bridget hesitated and plunked herself down again, exhaling a sigh. She stared at her hands, agitating her fingers into rotating patterns.

"I don't want to care," she said very softly. "I don't want to get hurt again."

"Aww, Bridge." Charlotte's gentle voice poured sympathy. "Sawyer would never hurt you, not the way Wes did. He's not anything like that at all."

Bridget had finally told her family everything about Wes. Charlotte was as sweet and thoughtful as always, not questioning why Bridget had taken so long, just understanding that the time for her to do so had to be right.

Her parents were still struggling with not being aware and regretting that they had not been able to help their daughter.

Bridget felt badly, but knew the emotions were theirs to get through and that she couldn't protect them from going through it, any more than they could have protected her. But she also knew that telling them, telling all the people she cared about and who cared about her—like Mildred, like Rena, and others—was absolutely the right thing to do, because misery and bad secrets thrived in the dark. It was only when you brought them out into the light that they lost their power.

Despite everything, she would never regret telling Sawyer first.

"I know he isn't," Bridget said. "He would never abuse me like Wes did, I know that. But he could still hurt my heart."

"Love is always a risk," Charlotte said. "Always. But only you can decide if it's worth it."

That evening, as Bridget flipped through her wardrobe, seeking an appropriate outfit for another bank meeting, her thoughts kept returning to what Charlotte had said. Was she willing to take a risk?

She only knew that, as hard as she tried not

to, she thought about Sawyer and Delilah, perpetually, naturally, like breathing in and out. She prayed for their happiness and healing. She wondered how Delilah was doing in school—if she had even made it back to school and if Sawyer had mended his way back into the family business.

She wondered if he ever thought about her.

But right now what she had to focus on was her final chance to impress the bank enough to agree to a loan for her. Dr. Burgess had made it clear that the potential buyers from the sporting goods store were nipping at her heels and that she had already delayed them for as long as she could.

As Bridget selected her clothes and laid them out, an unanticipated calmness overtook her. She knew without doubt that God was with her and, thanks to Sawyer Blume, she believed she had a great deal to offer. She was enough. If she never saw him again, he had given her that.

The next morning, the calm saw Bridget through a breakfast of a bagel with cream cheese and a cup of coffee. She was carrying her dishes to the sink when her phone rang.

"Bridget, it's Doc B here. I hope I caught you before you left for the bank."

A jabbing sensation rudely elbowed the calmness out of the way.

"I was heading out in about five minutes," Bridget said warily. "What's up?"

"Bridget... I don't know how to tell you this but, well, late last night I received an offer that I couldn't refuse."

Bridget remained silent, clenching the phone. She was happy she had renewed her faith, but wasn't it just a little soon for God to be pushing her to her limits again?

"It was exactly what I prayed for," Dr. Burgess continued. "It answered so many concerns for me."

"That's really great." Bridget found her voice. "I'm happy for you, Doc B, I really am."

She was happy for the doctor who had employed her and encouraged her to live up to her full potential, and with what Doc B was going through with her mother, she didn't ever want to be the kind of person who was bitter over someone else getting an answer to their prayer... even when it meant that her own prayers had gone unanswered.

"I'd like you to meet the new owner," Dr. Burgess said. "I just think it would help you to accept that I really have made the right decision."

Bridget had less than zero desire to meet the person who was going to disrupt Main Street with a huge chain store. She envisioned Green Valley being overrun with them and shuddered.

"Please, Bridget," the doctor urged. "It would mean a lot to me."

So, Bridget canceled her bank meeting with apologies and an hour later was waiting for Dr. Burgess outside the clinic. The autumn air was chilly and Bridget imagined it felt lonely between the final sighs of summer promises and the anticipation of Christmas wishes.

Dr. Burgess pulled up in her dark blue Ford and got out of the car.

Bridget hugged her briefly. "When will they be here?" she asked, her voice threaded through with tension.

"It shouldn't be long now." Dr. Burgess stepped back but kept hold of Bridget's hands. She squeezed them. "Bridget, I promise you, it's all going to be okay."

The wind lifted Bridget's hair and tossed it into an upheaval of waves.

"Bridget! Bridget!"

It was a child's voice but not one she recognized. She turned slowly in the direction of the voice.

Delilah Blume came hurtling toward her. "Hey, Bridget, look, we're back! Uncle Marc said that Daddy wasn't doing any good for the business moping around and Grandma said that she never wanted any of her boys to spend their lives doing work that made them unhappy.

Where's Sophie?" The little girl hopped and looked around. She wore blue jeans, a forest green hoody and running shoes. There was not even a glimmer of pink. "She's gonna be so happy I'm back."

"You're talking. She's talking?" Bridget raised her eyes to Sawyer, who had caught up with his daughter.

"She sure is. Isn't she *loud*?" Sawyer's laugh was shaky, as his eyes sought Bridget's reaction to their return, sought her forgiveness for the way he had left.

Her head was so scrambled she hardly knew what to say, or what to ask first.

"Your father?"

"He rallied," Sawyer said. "At least for now. He's about the toughest, most stubborn man I've ever met." But there was pride in his words.

"I believe that God granted us whatever time he does have left for us to mend things," Sawyer said. "It gave us a chance to talk honestly about many things. But Delilah is right."

"About what?" Bridget asked as her heart began to sing the first notes of a new song.

"I was doing a lot of moping around. I couldn't even bring myself to talk to you, and I hope you forgive me for that. I was afraid of what hearing your voice would do to me. I don't want to be without you, Bridget Connelly.

I want us to face the challenges of life together, not just as business partners but as life partners. Bridget, I love you and I believe that love will get us through whatever life brings our way."

"Bridget," Dr. Burgess said, beaming, "meet the new buyer."

"I didn't buy the clinic to upstage you," Sawyer said earnestly. "Your dreams and ambitions will always be something I support."

"I believe you."

Yes, Bridget thought, love was a risk but with all that God had already seen both of them through, it was a risk she now knew she was willing to take.

"I love you too, Sawyer Blume." She stepped into his arms for a kiss. When Delilah whooped with delight, she opened her arms to include the little girl in their embrace.

"I can't imagine life without either one of you," she said. "Let's go tell Sophie you're home."

"Home," Sawyer echoed, his smile a precious gift meant only for Bridget. "I like the sounds of that."

Epilogue

❧

On a beautiful, sunny afternoon in June, Sawyer waited with joy and anticipation for his bride to come down the aisle. His brother, Marc, stood by his side as his best man.

Almost a year ago he had told Bridget that their love for each other would make all the challenges worthwhile and now he believed it more strongly than ever.

After the wedding, he, Bridget, Delilah and Sophie were going to move into their new home together.

Their business was thriving and, best of all, Delilah had thoroughly enjoyed her year of school, played soccer, took up the clarinet and was a boisterous and happy little girl looking forward to whatever adventures awaited her in grade three.

The organ began to play the wedding march

and Sawyer's joy was almost uncontainable as flower girl and dog, Delilah and Sophie, walked down the aisle with the little girl proudly holding her leash. Delilah wore a blue denim dress—there would be no frilly flower girl dresses for his little girl—and Sophie wore a matching bow on her collar. They were followed by matron of honor, Charlotte, and by Tyson, who was again doing duty as a ring bearer, as he had for his adoptive parents' wedding.

Then there was Bridget, on her father's arm, a vision in white lace. But the intricate beauty of her wedding dress paled in comparison to the utter beauty that glowed in her loving eyes and in the sweet smile that was meant only for him.

As his bride made her way to him, Sawyer thanked God for bringing all things together for their good.

* * * * *

Dear Reader,

Writing and publishing can be a slow business and many things have changed since I first started writing this book.

But I want to talk about the things that don't change—the things that I have so much gratitude for: our Heavenly Father, the opportunity to tell stories that honor Him, and the chance to connect with the best readers ever.

You are all a valued part of the Love Inspired community and, in fact, we would not have a community without you.

Life can certainly throw curveballs at us, but, as I hope my story demonstrates, with faith, love and trust, we can rise above our challenges and pursue our dreams.

I love to hear from readers at deelynn1000@hotmail.com. I am also on Facebook. If you friend me or message me there, please do let me know that you read my book.

I hope you enjoy this story and remember that all the love and support you need is only a prayer away.

Love and blessings,
Donna Gartshore

COUNTRY LEGACY COLLECTION

19 FREE BOOKS IN ALL!

Cowboys, adventure and romance await you in this new collection! Enjoy superb reading all year long with books by bestselling authors like **Diana Palmer, Sasha Summers and Marie Ferrarella!**

YES! Please send me the **Country Legacy Collection!** This collection begins with 3 FREE books and 2 FREE gifts in the first shipment. Along with my 3 free books, I'll also get 3 more books from the **Country Legacy Collection**, which I may either return and owe nothing or keep for the low price of $24.60 U.S./$28.12 CDN each plus $2.99 U.S./$7.49 CDN for shipping and handling per shipment*. If I decide to continue, about once a month for 8 months, I will get 6 or 7 more books but will only pay for 4. That means 2 or 3 books in every shipment will be FREE! If I decide to keep the entire collection, I'll have paid for only 32 books because 19 are FREE! I understand that accepting the 3 free books and gifts places me under no obligation to buy anything. I can always return a shipment and cancel at any time. My free books and gifts are mine to keep no matter what I decide.

☐ 275 HCK 1939   ☐ 475 HCK 1939

Name (please print)

Address   Apt. #

City   State/Province   Zip/Postal Code

Mail to the Harlequin Reader Service:
IN U.S.A.: P.O. Box 1341, Buffalo, NY 14240-8571
IN CANADA: P.O. Box 603, Fort Erie, Ontario L2A 5X3

AN AMISH PROPOSAL FOR CHRISTMAS
Indiana Amish Market • by Vannetta Chapman

Assistant store manager Rebecca Yoder is determined to see the world and put Shipshewana, Indiana, behind her. The only thing standing in her way is training new hire Gideon Fisher and convincing him the job's a dream. But will he delay her exit or convince her to stay?

HER SURPRISE CHRISTMAS COURTSHIP
Seven Amish Sisters • by Emma Miller

Millie Koffman dreams of becoming a wife and mother someday. But because of her plus size, she doubts it will ever come true—especially not with handsome neighbor Elden Yoder. But when Elden shows interest in her, Millie's convinced it's a ruse. Can she learn to love herself before she loses the man loves?

THE VETERAN'S HOLIDAY HOME
K-9 Companions • by Lee Tobin McClain

After a battlefield incident leaves him injured and unable to serve, veteran Jason Smith resolves to spend his life guiding troubled boys with the help of his mastiff, Titan. Finding the perfect opportunity at the school Bright Tomorrows means working with his late brother's widow, principal Ashley Green...*if* they can let go of the past.

JOURNEY TO FORGIVENESS
Shepherd's Creek • by Danica Favorite

Inheriting failing horse stables from her estranged father forces Josie Shepherd to return home and face her past—including her ex-love. More than anything, Brady King fervently regrets ever hurting Josie. Could saving the stables together finally bring peace to them—and maybe something more?

THE BABY'S CHRISTMAS BLESSING
by Meghann Whistler

Back on Cape Cod after an eleven-year absence, Steve Weston is desperate for a nanny to help care for his newborn nephew. When the lone candidate turns out to be Chloe Richardson, the woman whose heart he shattered when they were teens, he'll have to choose between following his heart or keeping his secrets...

SECOND CHANCE CHRISTMAS
by Betsy St. Amant

Blake Bryant left small-town life behind him with no intention of going back—until he discovers the niece he never knew about is living in a group foster home. But returning to Tulip Mound also involves seeing Charlie Bussey, the woman who rejected him years ago. Can he open his heart enough to let them both in?

LOOK FOR THESE AND OTHER LOVE INSPIRED BOOKS WHEREVER BOOKS ARE SOLD, INCLUDING MOST BOOKSTORES, SUPERMARKETS, DISCOUNT STORES AND DRUGSTORES.

LICNM0822

HARLEQUIN
PLUS

Announcing a **BRAND-NEW** multimedia subscription service for romance fans like you!

Read, Watch and Play.

Experience the easiest way to get the romance content you crave.

Start your **FREE 7 DAY TRIAL** at
<u>www.harlequinplus.com/freetrial</u>.